PRIZE SURPRISE SWEEPSTAKES!

This month's prize:

A FABULOUS SHARP VIEWCAM!

This month, as a special surprise, we're giving away a Sharp ViewCam**, the big-screen camcorder that has revolutionized home videos!

This is the camcorder everyone's talking about! Sharp's new ViewCam has a big 3" full-color viewing screen with 180° swivel action that lets you control everything you record—and watch it at the same time! Features include a remote control (so you can get into the picture yourself), 8 power zoom, full-range auto focus, battery pack, recharger and more!

The next page contains two Entry Coupons (as does every book you received this shipment). Complete and return *all* the entry coupons; **the more times you enter, the better your chances of winning!**

Then keep your fingers crossed, because you'll find out by November 15, 1995 if you're the winner!

Remember: The more times you enter, the better your chances of winning!*

PRIZE SURPRISE
SWEEPSTAKES
OFFICIAL ENTRY COUPON

This entry must be received by: OCTOBER 30, 1995
This month's winner will be notified by: NOVEMBER 15, 1995

YES, I want to win the Sharp ViewCam! Please enter me in the drawing and let me know if I've won!

Name_____

Address _____Apt. _____

| City | State/Prov. | Zip/Postal Code |

Account #_____

Return entry with invoice in reply envelope.

CVC KAL

PRIZE SURPRISE
SWEEPSTAKES
OFFICIAL ENTRY COUPON

This entry must be received by: OCTOBER 30, 1995
This month's winner will be notified by: NOVEMBER 15, 1995

YES, I want to win the Sharp ViewCam! Please enter me in the drawing and let me know if I've won!

Name_____

Address _____Apt. _____

| City | State/Prov. | Zip/Postal Code |

Account #_____

Return entry with invoice in reply envelope.

© 1995 HARLEQUIN ENTERPRISES LTD.   CVC KAL

"You gave a marvelous performance of a girl madly in love."

"It was no performance," Celine said quietly. "I loved you, Guy. Never doubt it."

"Oh, for goodness' sake!" He swept that aside. "Let's get off such a maddening subject. It's a pity you don't go in for acting. You'd win an Academy Award."

"Does it have to be like this, Guy?" she asked.

"Tragic, but the answer's *yes*."

"You've changed so much."

"Indeed I have," he said coolly. "I'm holding you responsible for your actions like any other adult."

Dear Reader,

When I first thought of writing *Once Burned* I was reminded of an old saying to the effect that all families, happy or unhappy, are mysterious. Trying to unravel the mysteries, the ever-evolving sagas of family life, is the stuff of fiction. Family forms the fabric of our lives.

Families begin with love and marriage. Families come in all sizes, shapes and colors, levels of intelligence, tolerance and understanding. The *need* for family is probably the most powerful instinct of all. The ties of family, of blood, are so powerful they can be stretched to breaking point without ever giving way. Family triumphs in even the most tragic situations.

The greatest gift a parent can bestow on their child is a loving, stable environment where the solidarity of family, the *oneness*, the floods of love and loyalty form the mighty foundation on which the child moves forward with security and confidence on the journey of transformation to a well-integrated adult. The soul must be free to move on, to open up one's life to the future, to the wonderful possibilities that exist for those who **dare to dream.** It doesn't matter if one's dreams are never truly realized. The results of upward striving will make us happier, stronger, braver, more in control of our destiny.

I hope you enjoy *Once Burned*.

Margaret Way

Once Burned
Margaret Way

Harlequin Books

TORONTO • NEW YORK • LONDON
AMSTERDAM • PARIS • SYDNEY • HAMBURG
STOCKHOLM • ATHENS • TOKYO • MILAN
MADRID • WARSAW • BUDAPEST • AUCKLAND

ISBN 0-373-03381-8

ONCE BURNED

First North American Publication 1995.

Copyright © 1995 by Margaret Way.

This edition published by arrangement with Harlequin Books S.A.

® and TM are trademarks of the publisher. Trademarks indicated with
® are registered in the United States Patent and Trademark Office, the
Canadian Trade Marks Office and in other countries.

Printed in U.S.A.

CHAPTER ONE

EVEN on the plane Celine couldn't escape media coverage of her grandfather's death. The businessman in the seat next to her was reading a full-page obituary in the morning's paper: Millionaire Property Developer Dies. Centred was a large, smiling photograph of a strikingly handsome elderly man with piercing light eyes and an almost theatrical mane of snow-white hair. Sir Gerald Langton, Late Chairman Harcourt Langton, it said.

Celine turned her head away abruptly, fighting down the compulsion to burst into tears. Three years after she and her grandfather had parted in such anger she was heading home for his funeral. Home to her estranged family. Home to an enforced reunion with Guy. It would be impossible for Guy to avoid her, bound as they were by their shared history and the corporation.

Three years! Could it be *that* long? Her memories had the painful immediacy of yesterday. She had only to shut her eyes to be back in her grandfather's grand, dark-panelled office... She was seated, head bowed, hands clenched in her lap while her grandfather thundered at her for being a "hopeless little wimp" and an "over-indulged ninny incapable of taking up a brilliant challenge". His temper was legendary, but it had never been directed at her. Until *now*. And why? She had broken off her engagement to Guy Harcourt, for which in some form or other she would be punished for the rest of her life.

Her grandfather had doted on Guy. Guy was the
grandson of his late, lifetime friend and partner, Sir Lew
Harcourt. Real estate developers and builders on the
grand scale, the two men had been knighted by the Queen
in the '70's for their services to the wide community.
Guy's father, a senior architect with the corporation,
had been killed in an on-site accident when Guy was
twelve. The dreadful shock and pain of loss precipitated
Sir Lew's fatal stroke barely two years later. It was then
Gerald Langton had stepped in, becoming the young
Guy's mentor and male role model. Guy's devastated
mother and his grandmother, the formidable Lady
Muriel Harcourt, had allowed it for a number of reasons,
not the least of them securing Guy's future within the
corporation. He hadn't started at the bottom and worked
his way up. He had real power from day one. Guy wasn't
just talented, he was extraordinary. Not only was he a
brilliant architect and a visionary, he was a hard-headed
realist with a masterful grasp of business principles.

Her response to it all? She had fled him. At nineteen
going on twenty, product of an over-restrictive home life
and unsure of her own identity, she had lacked the confidence to cope with such a high-powered young man.
She only knew she loved him and that paradoxically
made things worse. She began to see herself in terms of
becoming a future liability. There was an immeasurable
gap between them. Eight years her senior, though he
never sought to dominate her, Guy possessed a ma-
turity, a natural strength and a toughness that put him
far beyond her.

It was her older, sophisticated cousin, Ashley, who
had finally put all Celine's anxieties and self-doubts into

words. "Let's face it, kitten. You're simply not woman enough for Guy!"

Once said it became central to everything. Guy wanted her. She wasn't such a fool she didn't know she aroused him, but inevitably as physical passion waned she could come to disappoint him. She couldn't have borne that. The truth of the matter was, she went in awe of him. Then, too, she feared being swamped just as her fragile grandmother had been pushed into a backwater by her larger-than-life husband. Her grandparents' marriage, outwardly serene, was actually a sham. A piece of theatre. They lived separate lives.

She had come to live with them when she was six years old and her parents had been drowned in a terrible boating accident. She could still remember standing in the hallway of Langfield looking down the long gallery at all the wonderful pictures. The colours were like *jewels*. She would have loved them had her mother been there to hold her hand, but tears weighed so heavily on her heart and in her throat she had lost her voice for months and her grandfather had to call in a special doctor to help her find it. Her mother and father were never coming back. Her grandmother told her they had gone to God. Surely God didn't need her parents to make Him happy? She hadn't liked God for a very long time.

Her grandmother, Helena, had always been kind to her, but her manner was so quiet and reserved the young Celine had often found her unapproachable. Her grandfather, so fierce and tall, with his rising loud voice, piercing blue eyes and crown of tawny hair that had once been red-gold just like her own, gave her everything he thought a child could want. She had heaps of expensive clothes, toys, the occasional companionship of a suitable

child. She was sent to the best schools. She took ballet
lessons, piano lessons, speech and drama. She was taught
tennis, riding and golf but no one could teach her to
swim. The most docile of children, she turned into a
little wildcat when anyone tried. Finally it was decided
the unfortunate situation was best left alone.

Until Guy. Guy had cherished her, overcoming her
deep-seated fears with his own brand of psychology. She
had loved him from the moment he had come into her
life, asking her grandfather was she the cherub who had
strayed out of one of Sir Gerald's Renaissance-style
paintings.

Guy, my love!

Even now that was the way she thought of him. His
beautiful ruby and diamond ring still swung between her
breasts like an extension of herself. She was conditioned
to losing the people she loved. She even *expected* it so
early had she been traumatised. Ashley told her, far from
being a "wimp", she was very brave for breaking off
the engagement. "I have to hand it to you, kiddo, you've
got more guts than I gave you credit for." Ashley with
her sharp wits and powers of observation always made
everything perfectly clear. Celine had a sharp mental
picture of them sitting in armchairs one lovely summer's
afternoon at Langfield watching Guy partner their
grandfather against Ashley's current boyfriend and her
brother, Michael. When Guy sent the deciding sizzling
ace down the centre line their grandfather had run to
him, encircling his shoulder. "Absolutely splendid, my
dear boy!"

"Touching, isn't it?" Ashley had flipped her an ironic
look. "Grandy dotes on Guy and doesn't Guy know how
to play up to him! You'd think Guy was the grandson,

not Michael. Grandy and Guy are two of a kind. Master manipulators. You're the iittle sacrificial lamb in the middle."

She might have made some little murmur of pain or distress but Ashley had continued, oblivious. "Of course, you're such a pure-minded little thing I dread to think what shocks lie in store for you. Guy's fond of you. No one can deny that. You're a sweet little thing...the way you look, the soft, enticing voice. But the bottom line is Guy is tremendously ambitious. He worked out the way to go on your sixteenth birthday. I spotted it immediately but you, the dewy little virgin, were blissfully unaware of it. The Harcourts aren't going to be manoeuvred out of Harcourt Langton. After all it was Sir Lew who put up most of the money in the first place. What better way to secure the top job than marry the sleeping princess!"

"Then why not you, Ashley?" Somehow she had found the courage to retaliate. "You're the glamorous one. Not me. You and Guy are more of an age."

Ashley had answered that, as well. "Not me, kitten. I'm much more of a handful than you. Not so easy to control. Besides, you're the one Grandy loves most, if he understands the concept of love at all. They don't call him Tiger Langton for nothing. Except for that, Guy would have made a big play for me. Surely you don't doubt it? Don't hate me, kitten, for pointing this out. I want to protect you. Put you on your guard. You have to stop playing the wide-eyed innocent."

Her answer was to run. Except, as she had come to realise, she could never run far enough. Guy was always with her. Always. She remembered the violent drama of the night she had told him she wanted out of the engagement. At first he had listened in total silence, his black eyes unfathomable, then her self-contained Guy had suddenly snapped, pulling her into his arms, telling her passionately he loved her and would never let her go. They were closeted in the library and he had shaped her body as he had never done before, kissing her so stormily she had almost fallen in a faint.

Where her strength had come from, she still didn't know. It took a terrible hour but she remained adamant she wanted the engagement over. She was desperate for escape. She could still hear her own frantic cry. "Guy, *please*, I've reached my breaking point!"

After that he switched off. Just like that. Adding weight to her shattering suspicion Ashley had been right after all. Then she had known nothing about real life but she had learned. Her grandfather, expecting her to buckle under, had cut off her allowance, but her grandmother had come to her rescue very quietly, giving her enough money to go interstate to find a place to live and look around for a job. It was her first chance to prove herself and she had. She had gone from playing the piano at the five-star Sydney Beaumont, to personal assistant, to the public relations manager. It was a hectic life involving setting up press conferences, photographic sessions, fashion parades, gala evenings, breakfasts and luncheons with celebrity guest speakers, but she took her job seriously and she handled it very well. She wondered how her boss was going to get on without her for a few days but Max was nothing if not super efficient.

Celine continued to stare fixedly out the porthole, lost in her sad reflections. At this altitude the sky was a gleaming washed-out blue. Beneath the jet airplane lay the thick woolly carpet of clouds. It seemed strange to

her Ashley hadn't been the first to ring with news of
their grandfather. Ashley was the only one who had remained loyal. Yet she had received the first shattering
phone call from Ashley's father, her uncle Clive. He'd
sounded as cold and arrogant as ever, talking down to
her as of old. She was expected to stay at Langfield. She
would be met by someone from the office.

*"It's time you started thinking of your duty like
everyone else!"*

It was grossly unfair but Clive Langton had always
been an abrasive man, deeply jealous and resentful of
Guy's importance in his father's life; anxious one day
Celine would inherit more than her share of the family
fortune.

The money didn't really interest her. It wasn't hers.
She hadn't earned it. She had learned to stand on her
own two feet. Besides Ashley had told her her name was
never mentioned from the time she'd left home. Ashley
kept her up to date on all the news, in the process un-
wittingly deepening the rift. Guy hadn't married, but he
certainly hadn't remained faithful to Celine's memory.
Just as Ashley had expected, he had made a play for
her, which she had scorned with the greatest of pleasure.
Ashley didn't have a high opinion of men. At twenty-
eight, stunningly attractive and an heiress, she hadn't
found that special man. Celine had found her special
man too early. And as a consequence she had lost him.

CHAPTER TWO

AT KINGSFORD Smith Airport an official met her and escorted her to the VIP lounge.

"Your friend is waiting for you, Miss Langford. A crowd of reporters is out front so we've arranged the private exit."

"That's very kind of you," Celine said gratefully, smoothing her hair. "Man or woman?"

"A gentleman, Miss Langton."

Probably one of her uncle's henchmen or even her cousin, Michael. She felt a little flurry of hurt Ashley wasn't here for her, but the situation was most likely chaotic. Her grandfather, apparently in perfect health and marvellously fit, had suffered a massive heart attack at home. Everyone would be stunned. She, herself, was grateful for the protection. She had no wish to talk to the press, much less fight her way to the car. She was back in the limelight as the "run-away heiress". An old photograph of her had appeared in another of the morning's papers under that caption. She looked amazingly wide-eyed and innocent. Long curling tresses. Little more than a child. She'd been engaged to Guy then.

The official held the door for her and closed it after him as she entered the room. She had endured a long sleepless night so her nerves were tight, but nothing prepared her for the sight that met her eyes. It was like coming face-to-face with an enormous ongoing trauma. She froze momentarily, but the man who had been flipping idly through a magazine threw it down casually and rose to his feet. Tall, immensely elegant, with a fine natural presence.

Guy!

She was pierced to the heart. She even made a soft little sound that signified pain. Whoever said time heals all wounds? Delusion. The ache was as fierce as yesterday.

For a moment Guy said nothing. He simply looked at her gravely. Finally, when she could bear his scrutiny no longer, he spoke. "Ah, the run-away heiress returns to the fold! How are you, Celine? You look shocked to see me."

"I must confess I am." She held out her hand, amazed her voice, though soft and gentle, sounded perfectly calm. "I didn't expect you, Guy. It's very kind of you to come."

"As to that, Lady Langton asked me to," he replied with exquisite brutality. Ignoring her outstretched hand, he bent his dark head and kissed her cheek, the merest gesture, yet it affected her fiercely.

He had changed. Though as achingly handsome as ever, there was a sombre cast to his expression. The sexual radiance so alive yesterday was masked by a brooding austerity. Where was the *sweetness* that had once hovered around his mouth? Gone with the flame of passion that had once burned for her in his dark eyes.

"What a lovely creature you are!" he remarked, the undisturbed calm of his tone telling her her beauty would never sway him again. "Obviously you didn't allow a broken engagement to ruin your life."

"Nor you, Guy." Sadness was in her voice. "I always wanted the best for you."

A gleaming irony shone in his dark eyes. "What a curious way you had of showing it. Never mind, it's all ancient history now. May I offer you my sincere sympathy. I know how much you loved your grandfather."

Her tender mouth quivered. "I really did."

"I know." His eyes seemed to stare through and beyond her. "*I* was the one who drove you away."

"*No*! Don't say that. I had to find myself."

The air between them was dark and glittering. "You couldn't learn about life with *me*. If it means anything to you, I think you look very poised and adult. That photograph of you in the *Herald* makes you look about fifteen years old."

"I was engaged to you then." She looked straight into his eyes.

"So you were! I'm always surprised I remember. I even recall the exact moment that shot was taken. The evening dress was green. It brushed your eyes with jade. I remember thinking at the time you were so *young*. The '*cherub*' I used to call you. No doubt *that* had something to do with your headlong flight away from me. There's a lot to be said for sticking with the same age group."

Briefly she touched his sleeve. "Please, Guy. Don't be bitter."

Some private thought must have angered him because he frowned. He glanced down at her pale hand against the dark grey cloth of his jacket and for an instant Celine had the sickening feeling he wanted to throw it off. "But I *am* bitter, my dear Celine. In fact I think you soured me on the whole female sex."

"It was never my intention." Despite herself there was a faint tremor in her voice.

"Forgive me, you ran from me as though I were Lucifer himself. I didn't lay a finger on you, either, except for the chastest kisses."

"I loved you, Guy."

"Oh, rot!" He gave a brief, mirthless laugh. "You feared love, Celine. Don't let's talk of it anymore. The whole thing depresses me. You know I suffer from the sin of pride. Still, we can't ignore one another while you're here. The family is shattered enough. Sir Gerald cast a long shadow. I suggest we behave civilly and we'll get through this testing time."

"That's what I want, too, Guy."

He showed absolutely no reaction to her words but turned his head as a porter tapped on the rear door.

"Ready when you are, sir."

"Many thanks. Coming, Celine?" He put out an arm. "We have a drive ahead of us. Some reporter is going to get wind of the fact we've left by the rear exit."

Minutes later they were seated in Guy's Jaguar cruising smoothly through the airport's environs to the open road. It was a glorious, cloudless day. Queensland's blue and gold.

Celine sat quietly, her hands folded in her lap. Only *she* knew her long nails were biting into her flesh. "I can't believe Grandfather has gone," she said finally, to break the silence. "I didn't even know he had a heart condition."

"He hadn't. No one was expecting it. Sir Gerald was in fine form. His death was typical. Attended to without fuss or delay. He spoke a few words to your grandmother. I believe, 'I feel strange,' and that was it."

"Now I can never tell him how sorry I am we parted in anger."

"Why would you *want* to tell him?" Guy asked, his expression quite daunting. "You've had *years* to do it."

"How cruel you are, Guy!" she protested. "You never were."

"If I'm cruel, Celine, you made me."

"I can only say again I meant no hurt. So far as Grandfather was concerned I was told he couldn't bear to speak my name or hear it mentioned."

"Who told you that?" He glanced at her sharply.

"Ashley. She's the only one who remained loyal."

"You think so?" There was derision somewhere in his cool tone.

"I know so."

"You always did champion Ashley. I never understood why. It always seemed to me Ashley was playing a double game."

"You couldn't be more wrong. Ashley has a brittle way about her, I know, but it's only a veneer. You never could see that."

"Or you're a real chump when it comes to Ashley. If she told you your grandfather couldn't bear to have news of you, she was lying. Most likely out of self-interest. Sir Gerald was furious with you. No one can deny that, but he couldn't hide the fact your defection upset and worried him."

"Then why didn't he get in touch with *me*?" Celine asked, unable to believe what she was hearing.

He flashed her a droll look. "You *knew* your grandfather, Celine. The first move had to come from you. That was his way. His natural inclination was toward despotism. But, generally speaking, benevolent. *You* had to make all the overtures. Actually he was proud you were standing on your own two feet."

"You amaze me, Guy." Celine shook her head. "I heard from no one. Not even my grandmother."

"Your grandmother, too, was always anxious for word of you. Of course she *got* it, but only through our contacts."

"I *always* remembered her birthday," Celine said.

"Darling, you never were a liar." His expression was one of distaste.

"I'm not lying now." Celine felt stricken. Ashley had been in charge of delivering the gifts.

He seemed to stifle a sharp response. "Let's leave it, shall we? In many ways this is going to be a very awkward time."

Celine stared out the window. The jacarandas were in bloom all along the hillside overlooking the river. "I won't be bothering anyone for long."

"No doubt you're anxious to get back to your boss?"

Celine's camellia skin flushed. "Excuse me, we don't have that kind of a relationship."

His near-black eyes swept her profile. "Whereas, Ashley, in typical fashion, suggested you did."

"Why do you dislike Ashley?" Celine asked, realising there had always been tension there.

"Don't get in a lather about Ashley. She's more than capable of looking after herself. I'm only repeating what she told me."

"Impossible." Celine's head felt tight. "Ashley knows perfectly well Max looks on me in the friendliest fashion. Much as he would a niece. It would do him a grave injustice to suggest anything else. I can only think Ashley was trying to pay you back in some way."

"Really?" Again the faint undertone of contempt. "And for what?"

"Perhaps for hurting me. I don't know. She always has been very protective."

"I'm sorry, Celine. That would take just too long to work out."

"Would you rather I hadn't come?" she asked quietly.

"On the contrary, I wanted to see how you've turned out."

He hates me, Celine thought. "I've been in control of my own life for some time."

"My dear, it shows!"

She gave a slight shrug. "And who were the *contacts* you spoke about before?"

His eyes met hers briefly. "Your grandfather always kept track of you. Be in no doubt about that. We have our people, Celine. They're necessary."

"Spies?"

"Let's say, minders."

"So there was always someone there watching?"

"Your grandfather very much disliked your stint at the piano bar. I think he was going to do something about it, only you solved the problem yourself. I believe the men gave you no peace?"

"Nonsense! I was well protected."

"Only you couldn't take all the attention?"

"Something like that."

"So rather than have you disappear, Max offered you a job as his assistant?"

"I'm very good."

"I'm quite sure you are. You never did have to prove yourself with me, or maybe you don't recall?"

She flushed, hating the reproach. It was justified. Guy had never criticised her. He had always been supportive.

Until *now*. "Uncle Clive rang me," she said in an effort to change the subject. "You know that?"

"Yes," he answered crisply.

"He sounded adamant I should come home."

"Of course. Where else could you be at such a time? I have to tell you, Celine, he still fears you might get more than he considers you're entitled to. He's acting chairman of the corporation in the interim and I expect he'll be appointed executor of the trust."

"I feel sorry for him," Celine said truthfully. "He idolised Grandfather even if they never did get on."

"I agree it wasn't a good situation, but your uncle has more prickles than a hedgehog. I find working with him extremely difficult. With Sir Gerald gone, I fully expect the situation to worsen. *Your* family like to forget *my* grandfather started the business. It was *his* idea: the bulk of *his* money. Sir Gerald was his best friend and invited along on the grand venture. You know the rest. Together they forged a business empire, each as valuable as the other, but in different ways. There's always going to be a Harcourt at Harcourt Langton, Celine."

She glanced at him quickly, hearing the thread of steel in his voice. "I'm glad of it, Guy. Are you saying Uncle Clive would like to see you out?"

"Darling, hasn't that been his main aim from day one?" he asked in a derisive voice. "Clive can't brook a rival. Naturally he has ambitions for Michael, too, but I regret to say Michael can't cut it."

"He never wanted to be part of the business anyway," Celine said. "Uncle Clive is too hard on him. Always was."

"Perhaps another instance of history repeating itself." He glanced again into his rear-vision mirror. "Someone is definitely following us. No doubt an enterprising reporter."

Celine gave a gasp of dismay, checking her own exterior mirror. "I don't want to be photographed, Guy."

"Why not? You look exquisite." Nevertheless he steered the Jaguar into a parking bay, turned off the engine and opened the door. "Stay here," he said briefly, his expression grim. "I'll go and have a word with him."

Celine couldn't resist a backward glance. A white Ford had pulled into the bay behind them. Guy had reached the passenger door and was tapping on the window.

She didn't wait for any more. She turned around, glad of her curtain of red-gold hair. The sun pressed warmly on the windows and she reached into her handbag for her sunglasses, slipping them on. She had been a private person for so long, this was going to be hard.

A few moments later she heard a car start up, then the Ford passed her slowly, the occupants staring in. A sharp-faced, dark-haired woman in her thirties who looked vaguely familiar drove, while her male companion, a heavy-set man with cropped hair, perhaps a photographer, sat in the passenger seat. She saw no more, because Guy rejoined her, sliding behind the wheel.

"They were tipped off, of course," he said, looking intensely irritated.

"To my arrival, you mean?"

"Certainly."

"But who on earth would do that? No one knew outside the family."

"What about your Max?" He pinned her briefly with his brilliant gaze.

"Max would never do such a thing." She spoke with authority. "He's my friend."

"So, forget Max. Who's left? Not Clive. Clive wants you under wraps. Nevertheless someone close to home gave them the tip-off. They told me. Hell and damnation!" Abruptly Guy broke off as the white Falcon cruising in the distance made a sudden U-turn and came speeding back in their direction.

"Duck!" Guy ordered shortly. "These confounded people just can't let anyone alone."

It was too late for ducking. The photographer was all but hanging out the window, snapping away rapidly with a long-distance lens.

"Blast them!" Guy was furious. "They never keep their word. Now there'll be another entrancing photograph to hit the papers. Ex-Fiancé Rolls Up For The Run-Away Heiress. There would have been more of a story had you actually left me at the altar. I'm only surprised you didn't. It would have appealed to your sense of drama." He leaned forward, switched on the ignition, showed his indicator and eased back into the traffic.

The suburbs peeled away in silence. They were heading for the city, and on to the opposite side of town. A sword lay between them. That couldn't have been more apparent. If she hadn't broken his heart, she had assuredly assaulted his male ego. Guy Harcourt, the brilliant young architect, handsome and dashing, a man who could have had anyone, thrown over by an undistinguished slip of a girl. She could feel the tension in his lean, elegant body, translated as it was into hard mockery.

She sought to turn it aside. "I haven't asked about your mother and Lady Harcourt. I hope they're both well?"

His answering tone was cool and measured. "I have to tell you they're no longer your fans. But yes, they're both well. Thank you for asking."

She swallowed because her throat had gone quite dry. "They love you so much they can't forgive me?"

"Something like that!" The handsome, sardonic mouth turned down. "After all, you gave a marvellous performance of a girl madly in love."

"It was no performance," Celine said quietly. "I loved you, Guy. Never doubt it."

"Oh, for goodness' sake!" He swept that aside. "Let's get off such a maddening subject. It's a pity you didn't go in for acting. You'd win an Academy Award."

"Does it have to be like this, Guy?" she asked.

"Tragic, but the answer's *yes*."

"You've changed so much."

"Indeed I have," he said coolly. "I'm actually holding you responsible for your actions like any other adult. After all that was between us, with the wedding only months off, you found you had to bolt. Why in heaven's name? You never *did* tell me. All I got was hysteria. And there was absolutely nothing I could do about it. The whole thing came as the most appalling shock." He glanced at her and a kind of lightning flashed from his near-black eyes.

She raised her hand to the gold chain around her throat. Whatever would he say if he knew she still wore his ring? Close to her heart. She seldom took it off. "I'm sorry, Guy," she said. "Maybe I was a little crazy at the time. I've always thought losing my parents so early and in such a way left me tremendously insecure. Everything was going too fast. Shatteringly fast. Grandfather was so thrilled and determined. You outstripped me in every way. I felt I had no real identity."

He made a sound that signified to Celine's mind, contempt and disgust. "At least you don't look the dewy innocent you were."

"That's what Ashley once called me."

"A dewy innocent? Compared to her, darling, you still are." His voice held that derisive note again. "A word of warning about Ashley. I don't suppose you'll listen to me any more than the old days, but Ashley is very jealous of you and no help for it."

"I don't accept that, Guy."

"Then you'll undoubtedly learn the hard way. I'm not speaking idly or because I've never liked Ashley."

She'd have fallen for it once. Dislike didn't preclude sexual attraction.

"You're outnumbered in your own family, Celine," Guy was saying. "I still care about that. Some habits die hard. The problem started when Sir Gerald brought you home as a child. I know he wasn't at all demonstrative, but he loved you in his own way. The rest of the family bitterly resented that affection."

The sun shone through the window striking red, gold and amber from Celine's long, curling mane. "It seems to me *you* were the one they resented. For that matter, the only time I got Grandfather's full attention was when I became engaged to you."

He looked grim. "I'm not going to deny he gave our engagement his blessing, but don't make a scapegoat out of me. Sir Gerald didn't relate to women terribly well. He was the ultimate male chauvinist. I'm not saying anything he didn't admit to himself. He never really relaxed in a woman's presence, for all he attracted them in droves. Men were the natural rulers. Women were only prized for their beauty. Don't you remember the way he used to say no woman is ever married for her *brain*?"

"I know I graduated with honours to no fanfare of trumpets. The only thing I really had going for me with Grandfather was the way I looked. I had his red hair. I had something of him. I didn't need a career. I didn't even have to mature. Grandfather thought a woman should be married young so her husband could mould her. And there, offering for my hand, a young god. *You*. It was a match ordained on Mount Olympus with Tiger Langton playing Zeus."

"But the Dream didn't come off."

"No," she said bleakly. "So what do we do?"

"Certainly not comfort each other." His tone was crisp. "I should warn you, you'll find your grandmother in a state of shock. I don't think she realises Sir Gerald has gone. In a way, he ruled her life."

"Guy, she had *no* life!" A little passion entered Celine's gentle voice.

"I realise that, Celine. I'm as much entangled with your family as you are. Sir Gerald overwhelmed her."

"So you grasp that?"

He glanced at her ironically. "Are you saying I overwhelmed you?"

"You did *then*, Guy."

"Well, we have to thank someone for giving you confidence."

The inference was unmistakable and she looked at him in sudden anger. "Ashley couldn't have told you Max and I were romantically involved. It's a lie!"

"Is it just!" His voice was light but cutting.

"Max is years and years older than I am."

"A father figure?" he suggested suavely.

"You're cruel."

"Perhaps a little. Your Max isn't as over the hill as your tone suggests. He's quite attractive. Not as fit as he should be, but he has a presence. I believe he's been married and divorced a couple of times."

She stared at him, unable to fault the chiselled profile. "Am I to understand you've had Max checked out?"

He nodded quite casually. "In the process of checking on you."

"Let me get this right." She moved in her seat so she could stare at him. "Grandfather did this?"

"My dear Celine, what did you expect? You've intimated you've learned a lot. Why not that? You surely didn't think he was going to let you disappear with no thought for your well-being?"

Bewilderment crossed her brow. "Ashley told me—"

"*Thank you*. I don't want to hear any more about Ashley," he bluntly interrupted.

"You don't realise Ashley has been my only friend."

He looked supremely unmoved, even disdainful. "Even *I*, your much-feared ex-fiancé had to find out if you were quite all right."

"I don't understand one word you're saying."

"Darling, I don't think you ever *did*. I would ask you not to upset Lady Langton with talk of birthday presents and the like. She has long since accepted you wanted no part of the family."

"That is totally untrue!" Celine defended herself strongly. "As I'm sure Ashley would be only too willing to testify."

"Ah, but then I don't find Ashley particularly trustworthy."

"But you're attracted to her for all that?"

He turned his head quickly, with a sharp, thoughtful look. "Is that what she told you?"

"No, of course not." Celine covered for her cousin loyally. "I'm just pointing out Ashley is a very glamorous woman. A surface hostility can often conceal attraction."

"Celine, you're still screwed up," he said. He spoke with cool, clinical precision. "I don't think I have ever looked in Ashley's direction."

"A great many people do." Celine stared fixedly out the window. "There's nothing to be gained saying any more. For both our sakes, Guy, it might be best if you leave me alone."

CHAPTER THREE

THERE were tears in Celine's eyes when they drove through the massive wrought-iron gates of Langfield again. Surely Grandfather would come to the door, autocratic face wreathed in a triumphant smile? With Guy most properly at her side, he would enfold her in one of his rare bear hugs, telling he'd always been certain she would see sense; how happy he was their long estrangement was over. His image filled her mind. Grandfather. *Grandfather*!

"Are you all right?" Guy turned to her, the most unexpected and devastating note of concern in his voice.

"No, I'm not!" she whispered. "I'm full of sorrow and remorse."

"Aren't we all?" he answered bleakly. "Pull yourself together, cherub."

The old endearment obviously slipped out. The next time he spoke, his tone was clipped and controlled. "As far as I know, your grandmother is alone, except for the help."

"Thank you." Celine looked and sounded very subdued.

He brought the Jaguar to a halt at the base of the stone steps but Celine remained in the car, staring up at the house. Now, no less than when she was a child, she found its imposing facade uninviting in the extreme. Langfield was her grandfather's vision of a gentleman's residence. Guy always said it looked like his old school.

27

High Victorian in concept, monumental in size, red brick and tile, a conglomeration of wings, gables, chimneys, verandas, arched doorways, even a square, turreted tower. Sir Lew, whose own plans had been politely declined, had once called it a "lofty monstrosity". Lady Harcourt went a step further and dubbed it a "hideous old pile". Nevertheless it was the sort of place "Tiger" Langton had wanted. Only the magnificent gardens, generously designed by Sir Lew, who hardly ever took offence at anything his friend would do, saved it. The great ornamental trees of the world graced its sweeping grounds. Jacarandas, poincianas, their branches weighed down by dazzling scarlet bracts, frangipani trees in a variety of colours, Indian laburnums, apple blossom cassias, tulip trees, silk trees, giant magnolias, their huge, goblet-shaped creamy flowers rising out of the shiny green leaves. The grounds were splendid with summer fragrance and colour; the famous roses everyone was allowed to see at a pre-Christmas garden party.

Except there was no Tiger Langton anymore. Celine, like her grandmother, was finding it difficult to grasp.

"We'd best go in," Guy said quietly. "I'll have a few words with Lady Langton, then I'll leave you in peace."

Celine pressed her head back and closed her eyes.

"What are you doing?"

"I'm trying to compose myself. Can't you see that?" Her eyes flew open, so liquid with tears they looked like shimmering lakes.

"Here, try my handkerchief."

It was snowy white, beautifully laundered, with his initial in the corner. Just like always.

"Have I done some baby-sitting in my time," he sighed.

"You mean, me?"

He didn't answer.

She dabbed at her eyes, leaving a few little streaks of mascara on the fine lawn. "Damn!" she said softly. "I'm sorry about that. Do I look all right?"

He gave a mirthless laugh, his black eyes moving over her. "The sad truth is you're more beautiful than ever."

"Beauty means nothing. That's all I had going for me with Grandfather." She took a breath, raised her arm to push back her hair, but a long strand caught on a link in her gold chain. "Aaah!"

"Here, I'll fix that." She heard the edgy note in his voice.

"No, it's all right." Nervously she tugged her hair away, using more force than normally she would have done. The chain flew up, exposing the ring pendant.

"Let me see that!" he said harshly.

Her expression held more than a hint of panic. "Leave it!"

"I think not!" He put out his beautiful, long-fingered hand, not caring in the least his fingers brushed the gentle upper swell of her breasts, causing a bone-melting rush of sensation. "My God!" he exclaimed. "Aren't there some mysteries in the world?"

And that was the truth. Colour came and went under her beautiful skin. "I put it on a chain for safety."

"Obviously the ring was worth more than the fiancé!" he said in a hard, ironic voice.

It could have been a showdown of some sort, so strong was the flow of emotion, only Ashley, looking glamorous in a fuchsia silk shirt and matching skirt, chose that moment to appear beside the car. She rapped sharply on Celine's window, a frown on her brow, intensity in her ice-blue gaze.

"Ashley come to check on us," Guy drawled. "She should have been a policewoman."

"She certainly seems anxious to talk to me."

"I dare say she's had a panicky moment wondering if we'd made it up. Personally I find her interference tiresome."

"*Please*, Guy." Celine checked to be sure the ring was inside the neck of the printed black-and-white silk blouse she wore with her Lagerfeld suit. Outside the car, unable to open a door because Guy had pushed a switch, Ashley's eyes were glued to the spot.

"Unlock the doors, please, Guy," Celine said.

"Sure. I was just giving Ashley a bit of aggravation." He put out a nonchalant hand and reversed the switch. Immediately the locks shot up and Ashley pounced.

"Kitten!" she cried, almost pulling Celine from her seat. "What the devil were you doing?"

"What? *What*?" Guy asked with hard mockery from the other side of the car.

"Guy didn't realise he'd pushed the lock button," Celine said. "How are you, Ashley?"

"Fine. Fine. I mean . . . shattered like everyone else." Ashley was still staring at some point on Celine's chest. "We'd better go up. Grandma has roused herself for the occasion. She's been out of it, I can tell you."

"With good reason surely?" Celine was dismayed by her cousin's rather callous tone.

"When she rights herself, if she ever *does*, she's not going to miss Gramps. Now there was one hell of a husband!" Her gaze shifted direction. "You'll stay for coffee, Guy?" In the sunlight her skin looked golden, her very thick blond hair worn in a straight shoulder-length bob, so meticulously cut not one strand marred the perfect arc.

"No thanks, Ashley." Guy walked on Celine's other side, his every movement full of the fluid grace of the fine athlete he was. "I'll pay my respects to Lady Langton then I must get back to the office. Several matters need urgent attention."

"Aren't we lucky you're there to handle them, darling." Ashley's narrow lips smiled, but Celine caught a flicker of something like hostility in the cool, blue eyes. On the surface there appeared to be no love lost between Ashley and Guy, yet both emanated a strong sexual magnetism. Both were experienced. Ashley had a string of affairs behind her. A lot of men, of a *type*, Celine suddenly realised, found her irresistible. Admired and chased after, perhaps it had always piqued her Guy had never been one of them. Or had things changed? They appeared unusually sensitive to one another.

Coming from the brilliant exterior Celine found it difficult to see inside at first. Then as her eyes adjusted, the paintings began to glow from the walls. They called up a wide range of responses. Pleasure, artistic appreciation, an involuntary desire to shift them around, change the dullness of the embossed wallpaper. But above all, the familiar feeling of loneliness and desolation. It would never leave her. She stood for a moment under the great crystal burst of the chandelier, the sadness of her expression attracting Guy's attention.

"Will the little girl never go away, Celine?"

She shook her head. "No. I'll never enter Langfield without remembering that six-year-old."

"You're lucky you had Grandy to turn to," Ashley pointed out. "You could have been an orphan."

"I'm indebted to him forever," Celine said. "And Grandmother."

"It's a shame, kitten, you forgot to thank her," Ashley said in a voice that ran with uncontrolled malice.

I should have known, Celine thought. *I should have known.*

There was a soft fall of steps on the stairway and as they looked up, a small, frail, elderly lady appeared on the first landing, the colours from the great, lead-light window spilling over her and patterning her dark lavender dress so it looked like she had thrown a brilliant multicoloured shawl over the sombre material.

"Grandma!" Celine didn't hesitate. She flew up the stairs with breathtaking grace, her face reflecting love, concern, sympathy.

"Dearest child!" Helena Langton put up her hands, then her face as Celine gathered the oh-so-fragile body to her, kissing the scented, paper-dry cheek.

"I've missed you, Grandma," Celine said, tears in her eyes.

"I've missed you, too, Celine. You'll never know how much."

"Where shall we go, Grandma?" Celine took her grandmother's arm gently, preparing to guide her down the flight of stairs.

"The drawing room, I think."

Ashley strode forward, looking as though she were about to clap. "I hope you don't mind my coming over, Gran? You were resting when I arrived. I didn't like to disturb you."

"I expected you, Ashley," Helena Langton said quietly, transferring her gaze to Guy. "Thank you, my dear. So very much. You're a young man of heart."

Unexpectedly Ashley gave a little hoot of laughter that sounded shocking in the hush of the house. "Some might quarrel with that, Gran," she said provocatively.

"Not me until the day I die." Helena looked at her granddaughters, but addressed Celine. "Would you mind going on ahead? I'd like a private word with Guy."

"Of course, Grandma." Celine drew a deep breath and turned back to the silent Guy. "Thank you for bringing me home, Guy."

He gave a slight bow that was immensely elegant. "I'll see you again, Celine."

"Of course it's unlikely he *wanted* to," Ashley remarked as they disappeared into the vast, crimson drawing room.

"You don't have to point it out." Despite the room's opulence and being crammed with valuable paintings and antiques, Celine always thought of it as rococo gone mad. Her grandfather had possessed such sartorial elegance, he had been famous for this dressing, yet his taste in architecture and decorating could only have been described as eccentric.

"Sorry, kitten," Ashley apologised, picking up a jade phoenix, one of a pair, and setting it down carelessly. "What on earth were you and Guy doing in the car?"

"*Doing*?" Out of Celine's gentle mouth came a tone that would have done credit to Queen Victoria as her most disapproving. "I don't follow you, Ashley."

"Hell, Ceci, it looked like he was fondling your breast."

"Don't get excited. He was helping me remove a strand of my hair from my gold chain."

"From where I was standing he got quite a kick out of it."

"I guess I did, too," Celine said sweetly.

"Really?" The superconfident Ashley sounded confused. "You'd be wise not to start any of that up again."

"I'm here for Grandfather's funeral, Ashley. I'm here, hopefully, to be of some comfort to Grandma."

"Good. It's about time!"

Celine moved to a sofa, sat down. "At least I can say I never forgot her birthday."

Ashley, who had been prowling restlessly, swung around. "Listen, I've got to tell you something. You'll find out sooner or later. Gran used to get so upset about you, I judged it best not to pass on any gifts."

"*Did* you?" Even as she accepted it Celine was sickened and shocked by the admission. Ashley in whom she had placed so much trust. Ashley who had exerted so much influence on her all the years they'd grown up. "How the mighty have fallen," she said quietly.

"I didn't want to hurt you, either!" Ashley cried defensively, perturbed by something in Celine's expression. A loss of grace for herself. "Try to see it *my* way. I was caught in the middle of a very difficult situation. Believe me, your running off to Sydney caused an uproar around here."

"Grandma gave me the money. *She* was the one who helped me."

"Don't think she came out publicly on your side. She never did cross Grandy. You were a taboo subject in this house. I was the one on the spot."

"You could have *told* me, Ashley. Instead you let me believe you were passing my presents and messages on."

"You know I've always been very protective of you, kitten. I had to keep your little sun shining. It seemed a harmless enough deception."

"I'm appalled, Ashley," Celine said. "I trusted you as my cousin and my friend."

"Do you have any idea what you're saying?" Ashley demanded. "I went down to Sydney many times to visit you. I listened to your problems."

"I thought you were the intermediary between me and the family."

"Kitten!" Ashley cried, and threw up her hands in frustration. "The family didn't want to know you."

"In fact they put a trace on me. Not that they *had* to when you were reporting to your father."

"Terrific!" Ashley said coldly. "Is this the best you can do? You come home for the funeral and immediately start a fight." She broke off emotionally and walked to the French doors, looking out. The perfume from the rose gardens beyond was amazingly heavy, even faintly cloying in the heat.

"I'm sorry, Ashley," Celine said, feeling sick and faint. "I'm just amazed at these revelations."

"What revelations?" Ashley spun back, anger in her face but choosing a quieter note. "All I'm saying is, I didn't pass on your gifts to Gran. I think they might have killed her. Her health is not good. I believe I was acting on the purest motives. I can see you're upset by it and I'm sorry it happened. We were always best friends, Celine. So far as I'm concerned nothing has changed." She crossed the room and sat down beside

Celine, taking her nerveless hand. "Has Guy been talking to you?"

"About what, Ashley?" Celine said, removing her hand slowly.

"About me, of course!" Ashley said disdainfully. "He hates me, you know. Under the suave charm he bitterly resents the fact I told him off."

"When he made a pass at you, you mean?" Celine's tone was unconsciously ironic.

"Not *pass*, dear." Ashley smiled bleakly. "He was hell-bent on an affair. With you gone there was only me."

"That doesn't sound like Guy." Celine shook her head. "In fact he gave me the impression I had wounded him deeply."

"God, you're incredible, Celine!" Ashley gibed. "Are you *ever* going to grow up? The only thing you wounded was his colossal ego. Let me assure you, you didn't in-spire undying love. Surely you've had more experience by now. Men simply can't be trusted. Don't get taken in by Guy again. He's not near good enough for you."

"I can't buy that, Ashley," Celine said, her smoky eyes full of disillusionment. "I'm sure you don't believe it, either. You were the one who told *me* I wasn't good enough for *Guy*. You made sure I understood that fully."

"Oh, Ceci, *please*!" Ashley implored. "You've been thrown off balance."

"I sure have!" Celine agreed, feeling a strong sense of betrayal. "I feel like the wind has been knocked out of me."

Ashley touched her cheek gently, making a soft, sad-dened sound. "Kitten, what can I do to make things better?"

"You can stop calling me *kitten* for a start," Celine remarked.

Ashley's expression registered disbelief, nevertheless she dropped her hand. "All right. What else am I supposed to call you? I've been calling you kitten since you were six years old."

"I feel it's inappropriate now. I'm twenty-three."

"Well, okay! I hope Ceci's all right?"

"You can call me Celine if you like."

"Precious, I don't want us to fight about anything," Ashley said. "I love you. I can never let *us* be estranged."

Celine looked directly into the ice-blue eyes. "For some reason, Ashley, I now doubt that."

"Then you're not thinking clearly," Ashley said in a strong, persuasive voice. "I blame Guy for that. You've always been under his influence."

"And yours."

Ashley laughed. "I am the elder by nearly five years. Be fair to me, Ceci, I've always looked after you. I used to stay with you for weeks at a time when you lost your voice. I've shared so much with you. All your confidences. I've told you so many things I would never tell another living soul. You know what that swine Alan De Burgh did to me. We've shared torrents of affection. Nothing can change that. Unless you listen to Guy. He's always had it in for me, for some reason."

"He has a funny way of showing it if he wanted an affair."

Ashley gave an exaggerated shrug, moving her straight, wide shoulders. "I didn't say he's not attracted to me in a weird kind of way. You know how these things happen. What makes it even more laughable is, I am attracted to him physically."

"A love-hate case, you mean?"

"Of course not!" Ashley said scornfully. "I know exactly what Guy wants and it's neither you nor me. It's Harcourt Langton. Surely you don't doubt that."

CHAPTER FOUR

CELINE and her grandmother dined quietly that evening. Afterwards, Mrs. Findlay, the very pleasant and competent housekeeper, served them coffee in Helena Langton's private sitting room, a pretty, comfortable retreat she had created for herself away from the overwhelming opulence of the main rooms. There were lots of books and flower paintings, a rather wonderful collection of Meissen figurines locked away in a Regency display case, the colour scheme of the spacious room soft and feminine in a mixture of pastels.

"I'm so grateful to have you home again, Celine." Helena settled herself in her favourite armchair. "It often seems to me you and I are the only gentle people in the family. The others can be so abrasive at times. *Hurting* people if you know what I mean, but then, my nature has always verged on meek."

"I *like* gentle people, Grandma." Celine passed her grandmother coffee in an exquisite cup. Beneath the quiet demeanour she realised her grandmother was deeply perturbed.

"I don't know quite how it happened," Helena continued to muse. "Gerald was always so hard on everyone. Always so demanding. He was never pleased or proud. Except of Guy. I think that's what wrong with Clive. He's always in such a *rage*! Nothing he ever did met with his father's praise. Even when he managed to do well, at school, at university, the business, Gerald's attitude was, so you *should*! I have a theory about my sons. Especially Clive. He couldn't hope to gain ascendency over his father so he sought to dominate the rest of us. It could be neurotic. What do you think?''

Celine was confounded at her grandmother's speaking out. "I think it isn't power in the sense Grandfather had it.''

Helena nodded, satisfied her views were being taken seriously. "I share the blame, of course. I was a poor mother. I didn't defend my children against their father as I should have. I believe they've always held it against me, but I was a very dutiful wife. A very dull and dutiful wife. I never had the courage to go against your grandfather in anything. I failed *you* in your time of need.''

Tears sprang into Helena's blue eyes and Celine leaned forward and clasped her grandmother's birdlike hands. They were heavily weighed down by diamond rings, one a ten-carat solitaire, *not* her grandmother, but a bauble that had attracted Tiger Langton's eye. "That's not *true*, Grandma,'' she said firmly. "You mustn't upset yourself any more than you already are. These things are in the past.''

"Ah, the past!'' A sad, ironic expression crossed Helena's pale face. "The past fashions us, dear. We can never get away from it.'' She slowly shook her coiffured head, short, thick and tinted a soft pewter. "I never thought *this* would happen. I thought Gerald would go on forever. Long after me. He was so vigorous. So bursting with life until the end. Even the way he went was typical. Swift and decisive.''

"No time for *me* to put things right,'' Celine said with deep regret.

"As to that, my dear, your grandfather was proud of you." Helena fixed her with large, clear, short-sighted eyes. "He wouldn't *hear* a word of you, but he checked on your every move. That was Gerald."

"Nevertheless I loved him, Grandma."

"I know you did, child." Helena picked up her coffee and took another sip. "I loved him myself though he virtually abandoned me after Nolan was born. Abandoned me to my own resources, that is," she qualified as Celine gave her a dismayed look. "There was no suggestion he would divorce me. Divorce wasn't on the agenda. We led separate lives, though we had *something* to start with I would have thought. I was considered very pretty in my day."

"You're still pretty, Grandma!" Although Helena habitually put herself down, she was, in her own way, a very elegant lady.

Helena smoothed the skirt of her silk dress. "I've looked after myself. I've had to. Gerald would have disowned me entirely had I not looked stylish. Of course I came from a good family, which was what Gerald wanted. But he was such a perfectionist, in the end he came to make me feel truly worthless."

Despite the fact it was the bald truth as her grandmother saw it, Celine was shocked. "That's *dreadful*, Grandma!"

"Dreadful to speak about it *now*." Helena looked past her granddaughter's glowing head, focusing on a painting. "But I can't help it. So many thoughts have been running through my head. Especially when I can't sleep. It's—what do they call it?—a *catharsis*. A kind of purging. Your grandfather's death has brought it all on. I can't pretend our marriage was a happy one. I can't pretend a lot of damage wasn't done. I need you *desperately*, Celine, at this terrible time. I need someone I love in my own camp. Gerald drained my last bit of pride and self-respect. No, don't flinch like that, it's true. I've kept quiet for a very long time, now I feel I'm going to break under pressure. Clive has assumed the mantle of head of the family in no uncertain terms. He is always courteous to me, but he talks to me as though I were lightly retarded.''

"When you're stronger, Grandma, you'll take hold."

"Do you think so, Ceci?" Helena looked wistful. "I'm no Muriel Harcourt. Now there's a woman impossible to ignore. Muriel has had to contend with the two greatest blows a woman can suffer in life. The loss of her beloved son, then the loss of dear Lewis. They were a *truly* devoted couple, not a couple of shams like Gerald and me. Lewis was a fine man, so full of kindness and integrity. Such *fun*! Your grandfather for all his abilities was never *fun*. Muriel faced tragedy so bravely. She has that inner strength, that capacity to rise above adversity. I've always been a very vulnerable person. Maybe it's biological? Who knows! I've been treated for depression as you know."

Celine shook her head. "I *didn't* know, Grandma." With her grandmother reaching within herself this could be a night for revelations.

"Oh, yes, for years!" Helena confirmed. "I must have seemed withdrawn to you?"

"You were always kind to me, Grandma." Celine bit down hard on her lip.

"Gerald would never have allowed me to become emotional about you, Ceci. You were Jamie's child. He warned me off."

"What are you saying, Grandma?" Celine's expression reflected her dismay and bewilderment.

"I've done, or rather *not* done, many things in my life I'm ashamed of, Celine," Helena said in a rambling, exhausted voice. "Yet I used to have good feelings about myself as a girl."

Celine's tender heart melted with love and pity. "It will happen again, Grandma. We'll make it happen."

"I knew what you were going through when you broke your engagement to Guy," Helena spoke more calmly.

"I thought I wasn't woman enough for him, Grandma."

"Nonsense. You were simply too young at the time. I *told* Gerald, but, as ever, my opinion didn't count. I was troubled by Ashley, as well. It seemed to me she wanted Guy herself. But Guy isn't at all like your grandfather, dear child. Not at all. Guy is not a cruel person. He's so *good* with everyone, including your poor grandmother. Guy is a young man who cares. You haven't ruined your chances with him, Ceci. He's never looked at anyone else."

"Are you sure of that, Grandma?" Celine searched her grandmother's tired face.

"I expect Ashley told you differently?" Helena asked with a grim smile.

"Not really." Celine wasn't prepared to reduce Ashley's standing in their grandmother's eyes even to the extent of not referring to all the little gifts that had never been passed on.

"You were always loyal to your cousin," Helena said. "My own view is, she may not be worthy of that loyalty."

* * *

Light rain fell during the night, but the morning of the funeral it was brilliantly fine. No tears from heaven for Grandfather, Celine thought. She slipped to her knees, praying for the strength to get through the ordeal that lay ahead. Her own feelings of grief and remorse she would have to hold in check. Her grandmother needed her to be strong. She would have to come up with some strategy to protect them both.

A few hours later she paced outside her grandmother's door still working on all the little tremors that racked her body. She had received two phone calls from her uncle Clive that morning. Admittedly he had worked very hard making all the arrangements but he was running things like a general. Her grandmother had refused point-blank to take calls from him. Less than twenty-four hours back in the bosom of the family, Celine could understand why. Clive Langton had an appalling manner. He had barked at Celine like she was some dim-witted subordinate. Only it was such an inappropriate time, she felt she would have told him where to get off. He had never treated her like a niece, a valued member of the family; more like an imposter who had somehow managed to gain a foothold where she had no right.

When her grandmother finally emerged from her bedroom Celine saw she was dressed in black from head to toe. She even wore a veil draped over her small black hat, something Celine only associated with royalty, but when she caught sight of Celine she put it back.

"I don't know how I'm going to get through this, Celine," Helena said, a statement made all the more piteous because she was trying to square her shoulders. Her small patrician face was lightly made up but her pallor was quite shocking.

"Then why *push* yourself, Grandma?" Celine went to her, kissing her cheek. "Is it absolutely necessary for you to be there? There's the family to represent you." Overnight it seemed her grandmother had lost *more* weight. Her expensive suit looked too big and too heavy on her slight frame.

"No, Ceci. I must do this properly. Gerald would expect it. I must carry out his wishes to the end."

"Then I'll be beside you, Grandma," Celine promised. "We'll get through it together. Uncle Clive said the limousine would be here at 10:30 sharp. He and Aunt Imelda will be riding with us."

"Dear God!" Helena moaned. "Clive defies any attempt to put him off. Arthur could have driven us." Her blue eyes slipped over Celine. "That's a beautiful suit, dear."

"Lagerfeld."

"Your accessories, too." Helena checked Celine's shoes and matching handbag with their famous label.

"You set a high standard, Grandma."

Surprisingly Helena blushed, instantly looking stronger and younger. "Where is your hat, dear? You'll need one."

"Good grief, I haven't got one." Automatically Celine touched her hair. She had decided against leaving it out. She had put it into a thick roll.

"Never mind, Goldie will find one for you. I don't want Clive taking you to task for not wearing one. He's so intolerant of not doing the done thing." Helena turned back to her bedroom, opening the door and addressing her long-time maid, Lily Goldsmith, who was in the act of scooping up discarded clothes and carrying them through to the huge walk-in wardrobe. "Goldie, dear, do you think you could find a suitable hat for Celine to wear?''

"No problem!" Goldie's still-keen eyes swept over Celine's graceful figure. "Give me a minute. I remember a very nice hat your grandmother never wore."

"Too *dashing* for me, I expect," Helena said.

Goldie reappeared almost immediately, holding a wide-brimmed black hat in her hand. It was perfectly plain, but very chic. The sort of hat favoured by the Princess of Wales.

Helena nodded her approval. "Go into the bedroom and put it on, Celine. It's a good thing you've done up your hair. If Clive told you 10:30 sharp, then 10:30 it will be. He's never early and he's never late. He's always right on the *dot*. That's his creed."

When Celine stepped inside the luxurious stretch limousine, property of the Harcourt Langton Corporation, Imelda Langton, a large, handsome blond woman, gave her a sharp, appraising look. "Isn't that hat a bit over the top for a funeral, Celine? I was thinking..."

They were not to hear. "The hat is *mine*, Imelda," Helena told her daughter-in-law in a surprisingly firm tone.

"It seems so unlike you, Mother." There was a malicious gleam on Imelda's sleek face.

"My father is being buried today, Imelda," Clive rebuked his wife sternly. "Why are you worrying about a hat? Mother has excellent taste."

Celine and her grandmother exchanged wry glances but Imelda, flushed of face, stared ahead. It was impossible for Celine to ignore the fact Imelda had always resented her, undoubtedly because of her special position in Gerald Langton's household. Moreover it had always been apparent he had favoured Celine over Ashley, something Imelda found quite incomprehensible. Photographers were waiting even as they arrived. What did it matter it was a time for grief, for family privacy? The media was having a field day with the passing of Tiger Langton. Clive Langton even held up a hand to the crowd. More like a knight on the way to an investiture, Celine thought, putting her arm through her grandmother's. A somewhat grainy shot of herself and Guy had appeared on page three of the morning's paper under the caption Langton Heiress Returns. Reading on it inferred to the arms of her ex-fiancé, the brilliant architect Guy Harcourt, grandson of the late Sir Lew Harcourt, co-founder of Harcourt Langton. Well, she was neither an heiress nor the woman Guy loved. So much for getting things right!

The cathedral Gerald Langton had never entered except for weddings was packed to capacity. Her grandfather would have been well pleased with the turnout. The sun poured through the magnificent stained-glass windows. The organ was thundering out some hymn Celine didn't know. Her grandfather's casket was up there before the altar, her grandmother's flowers resting atop it. Celine broke out into a cold sweat.

As they took their places in the front pew she caught sight of Guy's handsome dark head rising above the heads of his womenfolk; his mother, Eloise, a beautiful but retiring woman, and the formidable Lady Harcourt, a woman of considerable distinction. None looked her way. The service began...

At some point Clive Langton spoke, his strong, cultured voice resounding up and down the aisles and through the naves. Celine briefly opened her eyes. Clive's powerful hands gripped the lectern. His blue eyes, so like his mother's, had a fanatical gleam. The late Tiger Langton had been a saint no less. Not even Grandfather would have claimed that, Celine thought. She tried desperately to keep a faint grimace off her face, knowing she was in full view of the family and the great many dignitaries who had come to pay their last respects to a formidable public figure. Her grandmother was still gripping her hand. She could feel the trembling. There was worse to come.

At the graveside just as Celine thought they both could make it, her grandmother suddenly crumpled in a dead faint, causing instant panic, dismay, and an outbreak of conversation. There were at least a dozen prominent doctors among the mourners, including Lady Langton's own physician, who immediately took charge. Helena recovered consciousness almost at once but there was no question she could remain a moment more. Despite the fact her two sons, both big men well over six feet, hovered over her, neither thought to pick her up. Lady Harcourt advanced with Guy, giving him instructions to carry Helena to the limousine.

"You'll return with your grandmother, Celine?" Lady Harcourt fixed Celine with still brilliant black eyes.

"Of course, Lady Harcourt."

Alerted to trouble, the chauffeur brought up the car as far as he was able and Guy put the featherweight Helena into the back seat facing the driver.

"She shouldn't have come," Guy said very quietly to Celine. "She's not up to all this." His manner inferred the funeral had been arranged with too much drama. Something Celine couldn't dispute. "Are *you* going to be all right?'' He stared down into her face, shadowed as it was by the wide-brimmed hat.

"I hope so, Guy,'' she breathed. "I'm in enemy territory now.''

A great many people came back to the house. Food was set out like a banquet. There was alcohol in case anyone felt the need of it and most people apparently did.

This is crazy! Celine thought. Why do people do it? Was it a ritual no one thought to break? It was the *last* thing her grandmother needed or wanted, but there she sat enthroned in the drawing room, a small, frozen figure, while streams of people offered her their condolences. It was like some elaborate piece of theatre that had to be played out to the very end. Clive, as heir apparent to his late father, had taken on the role with relish. He appeared to stand even taller, his aggressive chin thrust forward as if to let everyone know they would have to contend with *him* now.

"Dad can't wait for the will to be read,'' Ashley observed dryly, coming up beside Celine, drink in hand. "Nothing is going to stand between him and the bulk of the fortune. God knows he's worked hard enough, copped enough abuse. There should be enough left over for the rest of us. Even *you*, kitten. I don't suppose even Gramps could die with *you* on his conscience. The little orphan.''

Celine turned her head, trying to cover her distaste. "If you don't mind, Ashley, I don't want to talk about money. Not *now*!''

"Oh, don't be so *precious*, Ceci. Everyone wants to talk about money. Even you. What I'd really like is to get my hands on Granny's diamond solitaire. Do you suppose she'd leave it to me?''

"Why don't you ask her, Ashley? I'm sure I don't want it.''

"More fool's you! It's *perfect*! It has no flaws and it has that tinge of blue. It looks quite silly on Granny's hand.'' She held up her own strong, long-fingered hand, the nails long and lacquered to match her lipstick. Like Celine, she was wearing a superbly cut black suit, its starkness relieved by a dramatic black-and-white silk blouse. Both young women had removed their hats and Ashley's blond hair swung around her face in elegant clean lines. She looked very sophisticated but she sounded very grasping. "Don't look now,'' she said, "but I think Lady Harcourt is coming our way. I'll skip, if you don't mind. Dear Muriel, worthy though she might be, isn't among my favourite people.''

"Nor you hers,'' Celine couldn't help pointing out.

"I just hope you're aware of *your* fall from grace,'' Ashley retaliated, looking surprised. "Certainly you caused the proud Harcourt family a good deal of humiliation.'' With that she flounced off as she had never done before.

Round one, or at least a strike, Celine thought. It was with a degree of trepidation, however, that she faced Lady Harcourt.

"How pale you are, Celine. Come and sit down with me,'' Muriel commanded. "Have you had tea?''

"I was trying to get a cup,'' Celine admitted.

"Well, then.'' Lady Harcourt eyed a passing attendant who hurried over. "Tea, thank you, and perhaps a sandwich. Black or white, Celine?''

"White, thank you."

"Black for me. Slice of lemon if there is one."

The attendant, a young man of girlish good looks, smiled as though he would move heaven and earth to find one.

"So, how are you, Celine?" Lady Harcourt asked quietly. "It must be very hard for you coming back at this time?"

"It *is*." Celine sat quite still, her face composed. "No time now to put things right with Grandfather. Grandma needs me, but I'm not so sure about the rest of the family."

"My dear, they've always been jealous of you. And Guy?" Lady Harcourt gave Celine a direct look. The same age as Helena Langton, seventy-four, she looked an astonishing sixty. Her curly dark hair, cleverly cut and tinted, still retained much of its natural colour, her dark eyes were striking, her olive skin in marvellous condition, her tall, upright body as slim and supple as a woman half her age. She was immaculately dressed, as always, but in a somewhat unconventional style. In fact Celine knew she designed most of her clothes and had them made up by an Italian woman who had once worked for the House of Chanel.

"I'm sure he will never forgive me," Celine said without a moment's hesitation.

"I've thought the same thing myself," Muriel freely admitted. "Do you have any idea of his pain?"

Celine bowed her Titian head. "It wasn't any fun for me, either, Lady Harcourt. I had to find myself."

"And have you?" Muriel Harcourt asked bluntly.

"What matters is, I'm trying. It's not simple. It's a life's task. I deeply regret the hurt I inflicted but marriage was impossible at that time. Guy had his mother and you: two women who adore him. I had no one.''

"You're dead wrong, Celine," Lady Harcourt said with a mixture of affection and impatience. "You had us. You could have come to us. We were friends."

"Of course. I want more than anything for that to still be the case, but I was deeply emotional at the time and not thinking clearly. I realise I behaved badly and I've been punished."

"We've all been punished, dear," Lady Harcourt said wryly. "These things happen, now we must seek to repair the damage. I always did feel for you, Celine. Indeed I spoke out for you from time to time, which Gerald didn't like. He couldn't tolerate any kind of advice. He used to sit there fuming because unlike with other people he couldn't blow his top. The most complete autocrat, Gerald. He won't mind my saying it. Eloise and I were deeply upset when you broke off the engagement. I'm sure you'll understand that. Had you come to us before you took off..."

"You must know what it's like to be under too much pressure, Lady Harcourt," Celine argued. "I was too young, too vulnerable, too *ordinary* for Guy."

Lady Harcourt showed her disbelief in an ironic bark. "You were too young certainly, inexperienced in the ways of the world, but *ordinary*? Never! You're an exquisite-looking creature, Celine, as you must know. I know you have little vanity but you do have eyes. You still have your sweet nature and if your grandfather failed to notice your charm and high intelligence, it wasn't lost on any of us, particularly my grandson. Calling yourself ordinary simply won't do!"

"I felt I was *then*," Celine said with the ring of truth. "I never did quite believe it, you know."

"What, dear?" Lady Harcourt turned slowly to stare at her.

"That Guy loved me. That he wanted to marry me. I found it a mystery."

"I can promise you it *wasn't*. Nor did it have anything to do with your being a Langton," Lady Harcourt added grimly. "There were others, of course, to reinforce your sense of insecurity?"

"No." Celine denied it, her face troubled.

Lady Harcourt gave her bleak laugh again. "I don't accept that, Celine. I do have intimate knowledge of the family. It's not going to be easy for you."

"I won't be staying." Celine half expected Lady Harcourt to draw a sigh of relief. "When Grandma feels stronger, I'll go back to Sydney. I have an interesting job there."

Lady Harcourt stared at her with those acute black eyes. "Celine, you'll have to think of something else. You'll have a substantial inheritance."

"By no means a foregone conclusion, Lady Harcourt."

"Call me Muriel, dear. I can't think why you're persisting with this Lady Harcourt."

Surprised, Celine gave her lovely, spontaneous smile. "Are you sure?"

"Of course I'm sure. It will be a good experience for us both. We were *almost* family, Celine. No matter what, there'll always be something between us. You do realise you won't be able to go back to Sydney. Helena will have need of you. Gerald's death has sapped all her strength."

"I'm thinking she might collapse again at any moment."

"She shouldn't be sitting there," Lady Harcourt agreed. "She looks so frail and wretched."

"She *insisted*, Muriel. There was nothing I could do. Grandma has started making her own choices."

"I'm not criticising you, dear. Helena has steel in her. She'll find it yet. God rest Gerald's soul, but he was such a domineering man. You all suffered because of it. Helena was terribly affected. She was such a bright, pretty girl. Very appealing. Gerald wanted to seal her up in a display case. No one can survive that. More than anything she'll need your support and love. The rest of the family would have to be described as confrontationist. No, you can't think of going away, Celine."

"I would have thought you'd want me to go away?" Celine looked at Lady Harcourt very seriously.

"My dear girl, *why*?"

Celine shrugged, a slight movement of her delicate shoulders. "For Guy's sake. He met me at the airport as you know. A gesture to Grandma. He made it clear he didn't enjoy seeing me again."

"You surely didn't expect him to welcome you with open arms?" Muriel Harcourt said. "Being jilted is a good enough reason for feeling bitter."

Celine lowered her eyes and a flush spread across her creamy skin. "I didn't jilt Guy. I was totally overawed by him."

"You certainly didn't show it," Muriel maintained. "Good heavens, I never saw any two people more deeply in love. You sparkled in one another's company."

"I thought he was being propelled into it."

"Then think again, Celine," Muriel said sternly. "We can't change the past but if we're wise we try for reconciliation. Take it from a woman who *knows*. Guy did love you. I can't speak for his feelings now. He has rather gone into his shell." She paused as the attendant approached them bearing a tray. "Eloise will want to speak to you before we go. We both welcome you back."

"Thank you, Muriel."

Lady Harcourt leaned over and patted her hand. "Generally speaking, dear, yours is not a happy family. You'll need our support."

The reading of the last will and testament of Gerald Connor Langton was scheduled for 6:00 p.m. in the library. Henry Fowler, senior partner of the prestigious law firm of Fowler, Mortensen & Spencer, a firm that had served the family for over forty years, had been appointed trustee and executor and as such would conduct proceedings.

The family began to arrive a good half hour before the reading was due to commence. Celine stood behind the curtain in her grandmother's bedroom relaying information as it came to hand. Helena, fully dressed, was lying on the bed, a hand over her eyes.

Celine looked down at the party disembarking from a brand new, top-of-the-range Mercedes. "It's Uncle Clive and Imelda. I don't know whether to laugh or cry. Aunt Imelda is wearing a bright red dress."

"Triumph!" Helena said. "The children with them?"

"Yes, Ashley and Michael. They've grown very much alike. Yet the sad thing is they're not close."

"There's something about Ashley that reminds me of Gerald," Helena murmured.

"Uncle Nolan is arriving now."

"Do you know they call Dorothy 'Lofty' behind her back? It's her overbearing manner, of course. She's only five feet three."

"Dana and Harris are with them." Celine parted the curtain a little, staring down onto the drive. "Does Dana have a job yet? I didn't like to ask."

"Dana is a professional young socialite," Helena replied. "Apparently it's very demanding of her time. Poor old Harris inherited Gerald's famous red-gold mane, as you did, but unfortunately none of his brain or his striking good looks. Harris has been in and out of trouble since his kindergarten days. When he's finished university, if he passes his exams, he'll go into the business. Goodness knows in what capacity."

"I think he's fighting to find some sort of identity," Celine said. "Of all us grandchildren Ashley is the only one oozing self-confidence."

"And yet she never did anywhere near as well as you with your studies. Neither is she as beautiful. There's a cunning mind behind Ashley's smooth face, Celine. She would fight just as ruthlessly as Gerald for what she wanted. You're older now. I know you're going to be able to cope."

Celine turned away from the tall windows. "You seem to be warning me against Ashley, Grandma."

Helena struggled up from the bed. "I'm letting my instincts roll. They've always been operational. I just never expressed myself, that's all. Smooth my hair for me, would you, please, darling, then we must go downstairs. I have a feeling this will is going to break a lot of hearts."

When they reached the richly appointed library, they found the family scattered about in chairs. Clive got up immediately from behind his late father's splendid desk and went to his mother, inquiring after her well-being. She went to assure him she was quite all right but Clive had already turned away, gesturing to his son, Michael, to get up so Helena could have a central seat. The large room was chock-a-block with armchairs and tables, great globes on stands, high reading tables and a vast collection of books on every conceivable subject, most of them untouched by anyone outside of Celine who, as an extremely lonely and isolated child, had become an inveterate reader.

"We'll have to get that portrait of Gramps down," Ashley said from the depths of a comfortable winged-back chair. "It's giving me the shivers. Didn't he have the most *piercing* regard?"

"It always made *me* miserable," the young, lanky Harris volunteered. "One glare from Gramps was worse than six of the best."

"Had you ever behaved yourself you wouldn't have needed six of the best," Clive Langton rebuked his nephew, who blushed furiously. "What's keeping old Henry?" he demanded in a highly irritated tone. "*I'm* always punctual."

"Obsessively so," Nolan commented promptly, angry Clive had usurped the parental role of correcting Harris.

"It's not six yet, Clive," Helena pointed out mildly. "I do wish you would sit down again. All this raging is going to lead to a heart attack or stroke."

"Well, *thank you*, Mother." Clive collapsed into an armchair, looking surprised and aggrieved. "I really think Henry's getting past it. No one actually goes to him anymore. Now that Father's gone I think it's high time we found ourselves a new firm of lawyers.''

"If Henry and his firm were smart enough for your father, they're smart enough for anyone," Helena said, her soft voice actually scratchy. "Surely that's Henry's car now?"

"Who else drives a broken-down Rolls?" Ashley asked derisively.

"I thought it was faultlessly maintained," Celine answered out of loyalty to Henry. Not only was it true, Henry, a courtly gentleman, had always been very kind to her.

"It's as old as the hills, Ceci," Ashley said carelessly.

Moments later Henry was shown in by Mrs. Findlay, ghostly grey beside the sheer drama of the young man who accompanied him.

Guy! Celine's heart leapt. He looked almost unbearably handsome in the black suit he had worn to the funeral, dark, dangerous, aroused. At the expression on Clive's face, his splendid head snapped up. Almost like a mettlesome charger, Celine thought.

Clive, a big, overweight man, crushed Henry's elderly fingers then demanded of Guy what he was doing here. Guy ignored him, went to Helena, bent and kissed her cheek, while she put up a hand to touch his.

"What the hell is going on here?" Clive was breathing deeply, his handsome florid face flushed a deep red. "This is a *family* reading."

"It would seem, Clive, I'm one of the beneficiaries," Guy said in his beautiful, dark timbred voice. "The will will explain. I hadn't intended coming, certainly not without speaking to Lady Langton, but Henry rang me and managed to change my mind. I had an appointment

I was committed to late afternoon so there's been little time."

"Please sit down, Guy." Helena indicated a chair beside Celine. "You're always welcome in this house. It's still *mine*, I believe."

Clive looked stupefied. "I think you'd better get on with it, Henry," he snapped.

"All in good time, Clive." Henry went behind the desk, placing his briefcase on the top.

"May I be the first to congratulate you for getting in Gramps's will." Ashley leaned forward, treating Guy to a blue, glittering stare of challenge.

"Nothing is simple and straightforward, Ashley," he told her suavely. "I think you'll find I'm stealing nothing from you."

"Good on you, Guy!" Harris lifted a glass of ginger ale to Guy then set it aside. Harris admired Guy more than anyone he could think of. Guy had helped him so much with his studies. Guy never made him feel the next best thing to a brain dead moron. That was the way his cousin Ashley had always treated him. He gave Guy and Celine a broad, beaming smile. They were impossibly beautiful people, both of them. He was really very pleased to see Ceci back. Ceci had never treated him like a total dolt, either.

"Take that stupid grin off your face, Harris," his mother, Dorothy, admonished him, showing her irritation while his father sat, eyes locked tight, brow furrowed as though trying to fathom the complexities of the human condition.

"Dear Dorothy! Always keeping herself busy putting somebody down," Guy murmured to Celine sotto voce.

"I bet you're thrilled to be back in the bosom of the family."

In truth she was immensely glad to have him there beside her. Even a hostile Guy radiated strength for her. Once he had been her true love, her dearest friend, her greatest ally. She must have been *mad*! No woman in her right mind would have fled Guy. No wonder her grandfather had called her a wimp. Seen from his eminence, he might even have doubted her sanity.

Henry had opened his handsome leather briefcase, but to the varying degrees of astonishment of everyone present, instead of withdrawing a great sheaf of papers he placed a black videotape on the desk.

"For God's sake!" Clive burst out, then hastily stifled the rest.

Celine turned in total dismay to seek Guy's brilliant, black eyes.

"Surely you didn't think Tiger Langton would just *disappear*?" he asked in a dry, ironic voice.

"Oh, Guy!" Her sigh was soft and desperate. Like her grandmother, she felt exceedingly frail.

"Hang in there, cherub." The severity of his expression amazingly softened. "It could be worth your while."

"Isn't this just *ghastly*!" Ashley demanded of the room in general. "Surely Gramps isn't going to *talk* to us?"

"It looks alarmingly like it." Imelda began to fan herself though the house was airconditioned. The rest of the family sat like a school of fish, mouths agape, but Helena looked like she was going to slip from her chair to the floor.

Celine sprang up and went to her. "Grandma, are you all right?" she asked anxiously.

"Why didn't I *know* this is exactly what Gerald would do?" Helena moaned. "Even when he's dead he won't lie down."

"Bear with me a moment," Henry appealed to them, looking around him almost absent-mindedly.

"To the right of you, Henry," Guy called. "The large antique cabinet. It houses the TV and video equipment. I'll fix it for you if you like."

"Thank you, dear boy!" Henry looked towards Guy gratefully. "I know I should be up with all these gadgets, but I'm not."

Shockingly, Ashley laughed, a caustic sound, and her father rounded on her, his favourite, but not beyond the cutting edge of his tongue. "If you can't behave in a seemly manner, Ashley, I suggest you go outside."

"Sorry, Dad," Ashley apologised, very meekly for her.

While they all watched in trepidation, Guy set the TV to the appropriate channel, then pushed in the video.

"Now this dreadful, dreadful day is complete," Helena announced in her most dismal tones.

"Amen." Guy glanced keenly at Celine's pale profile, then briskly in the manner of a doctor took her nerveless hand.

Sir Gerald Langton's splendid image came up on the screen. He was seated behind the desk in his grand, dark-panelled office, his expression more sardonic than ever.

"My dear family," he began in his unforgettable voice.

For close on thirty minutes they sat transfixed while Gerald Langton detailed what he wanted done with the family fortune. He spoke to them in turn, but not to complete silence. The deep, authoritarian tones were accompanied by intermittent outbursts of horror, anger, shushes and moans.

There were shocks galore!

Helena, shoved into a backwater all her life, was placed at the virtual mercy of her eldest son, Clive, who would inherit the house and all its contents except the art collection, which would go to Celine as "the only one who knows how to appreciate it," a claim howled down by Clive, Imelda and Ashley in unison. Helena was assured she would be maintained in customary style and her every wish fulfilled. It was obvious Gerald Langton believed Helena would continue to reside at the house after her son and family moved in. It was, after all, an extremely large house.

"How appalling!" Celine edged closer to Guy, quite shocked.

He nodded. "Even to the end Gerald left Helena grief. Clive will take his responsibilities seriously, but at what cost? It's just as well Helena has her own money."

Even Ashley had the grace to take her grandmother's part. "God, isn't that bizarre! Gramps really was the ultimate male chauvinist. Didn't he think Granny could manage her own life?"

"I hope you're not inferring I can't look after Mother, Ashley?" Clive glowered.

"I *know* you will, Pops. But Granny really should have been left the house in her lifetime. I don't want to live in this old museum. I don't imagine Celine will want to live with us, either."

"Of course not!" Harsh colour in her cheeks, Imelda made her position clear. "You won't know the place after I turn my attention to it. It could be splendid if we clear out a lot of the junk."

"You have my permission, Imelda, to go to work," Helena said, demonstrating she couldn't have cared less.

"So Imelda's in charge now and your grandmother is out in the cold," Guy murmured darkly. "Don't you just love it!"

Clive, as the eldest son, the rightful heir, was addressed next.

"This is a farce!" he cried once, as his late father tore his hopes and ambitions apart. "Who gets the yacht and the Lear jet?"

"I wonder, Clive, if you wouldn't mind keeping your comments to the end," Henry pleaded in vain. He remembered now his late client had always said Clive had "more energy than brains". Clive was on his feet now, fists clenched, reminding Henry strongly of a wounded bull about to charge.

Nolan was equally dissatisfied and perplexed, though he retained his seat. When Gerald addressed his two grandsons, Michael and Harris, words to the effect "too much too soon could only ruin young men", Harris broke into near hysterical laughter when told he had inherited his grandfather's collection of gold cufflinks. To add to the aggravations Clive told him not to keep acting the fool.

"Isn't that a case of the pot calling the kettle black?" Guy murmured into Celine's ear. Signals were passing rapidly from one to the other, much as in the old days for all the unhappy state of their relationship. The library was thrumming with shock and ill feeling.

The granddaughters were next. Ashley, Celine and Dana, who was praying she wouldn't have to wait for her windfall like her brother. Ashley was given the string of glamour racehorses in recognition of her love and knowledge of horses and racing, something that delighted her, a luxury unit in Sydney, another on the Queensland Gold Coast and a sum of 10 million dollars free of tax.

"That means I can take off when I feel like it," Ashley said.

Dana, the youngest, unexpectedly came next. Dana inherited the Meissen collection, her grandfather's apartment overlooking the Queensboro Bridge in New York and 10 million dollars free of tax.

"I can't wait to beat it to the Big Apple!" Dana said with a wild grin.

"I'll choose the time you're going there!" her mother thundered, looking on the bequest as a calamity. She needed her children to depend on her for survival.

When Celine's turn came, she tensed then sat straight, prepared for anything. Or nothing. There was nothing her grandfather had enjoyed more than being unpredictable. Gerald Langton began by expressing his regret he had "probably" driven her away, nevertheless, his handsome face deeply serious and frowning, he assured her he still loved her and was immensely proud she had demonstrated she could stand on her own two feet. He was now giving her a portion of his Harcourt Langton shares equal to that of her uncles, twenty percent. She had a seat on the board, various properties including a tea plantation in North Queensland, a hotel in Fiji and the sum of 10 million dollars tax free. She was also to receive the art collection with the exception of the Renoir, which was to go to Lady Muriel Harcourt because she had always loved it.

"This is monstrous!" Clive cried, sagging back in his armchair. "What's the world coming to! Father was a complete mystery to me."

Celine turned to Guy, who was looking very hawkish. "For once I agree with Uncle Clive."

"Why do you say that? You *were* his favourite grandchild."

"The trouble is, he's got several."

"It's hard to feel sorry for them," Guy drawled. "Cheer up, darling Ashley will try to contest the will herself. I wouldn't put it past her. My sympathies are entirely with your grandmother. I have it on very good authority, her *own*, she'd as soon reside on the other side of the moon as with either of her sons. In fact if we don't get her to bed she'll finish up in intensive care."

"I've waited too long already." Celine stood suddenly and was waved down very politely by Henry. "This won't be long now, dear. There are bequests to friends, staff, various charities your grandfather supported, but they are contained in the typewritten copies of the will. Guy is the last one to be mentioned." He released the stop button on the video recorder and Sir Gerald started to speak.

Now it was discovered the fate of the yacht and the Lear jet. Both were left to Guy in recognition of the fact he was the best yachtsman among them and he actually held a licence to fly the jet. Guy also inherited all the shares in a fledgling property company GLRealty, based, in Clive's words "in the Never Never", which his more knowledgeable father had known was coming closer every day. The collection of Rodin sculptures, Sir

Gerald's famous set of golf clubs, and all the volumes on architecture in the library.

"As I recall, a lot of them were my grandfather's," Guy told Celine, keeping his voice low. "Sir Gerald borrowed them and forgot to give them back."

"Guy, you're awful!" She had an impulse to laugh, knowing he was similarly affected.

"I know. You used to love it!"

The greatest shock was to come, intensifying the feelings of outrage that so choked the room, and Celine, for one, had difficulty breathing. Guy was to receive fifteen percent of Sir Gerald's shares in Harcourt Langton, which with Guy's own shares inherited from his grandfather gave him the same clout as Clive and Nolan put together. Something their father would have seen only too clearly.

Sir Gerald faded on a challenging note as though he privately believed he would outlast the lot of them.

"My God!" Clive cried in despair. "Robbery! I'm sure I would never wish Father to go to hell, but this will is a perfect *swine!*"

"Which was often said of Sir Gerald." Guy stared into Celine's misty grey eyes. "Don't you just wish you'd married me now? Our combined shares give us control of Harcourt Langton."

She flinched a little at the heavy irony. "I'm not so dumb I can't add up."

"I never thought you were dumb, either, but as it's turned out it seems you were. I suppose this will make me a lot more attractive to Ashley, as well." His brilliant eyes were full of a black humour.

"If only she'd received my share you'd be just right."

"There's that," he considered, his handsome mouth sardonic. "On the other hand I've found it best to do my own thing. Depend on me, darling, to take control *without* you."

CHAPTER FIVE

"GET me a brandy, darling, to settle my tummy," Helena implored, her mood becoming more melancholy by the minute. "If I were any sort of a drinker, which I may well become, I'd say make that a double."

"Get into bed, Grandma," Celine said, turning back the covers and plumping the pillows. "Come on, now. No more dilly-dallying. Too much has been expected of you."

"What me, the *nobody*?" With a sigh Helena gave in, going to her brass four-poster bed adorned with a blue canopy and allowing Celine to tuck her in. "I have to say this, my family, with the exception of you and possibly Harris, are a shocking lot. Every last one of them was left a fortune but whenever they turn up they're full of complaints. Really, I was disgusted with them tonight. So you and Guy got a lot more than anyone expected? That's rough! I, Gerald's wife for more than fifty years, have been treated like a baby."

Celine put out a hand and smoothed her grandmother's hair from her forehead. "I'm sure Grandfather didn't mean to hurt you," she offered wretchedly. "It's as Ashley says..."

"Please don't mention Ashley," Helena said, the same smooth forehead creasing into a frown. "I hope you realise now, Celine, just how jealous she is of you."

"She has an excuse, Grandma."

"If she's smart enough she won't cross you, but I have the dismal feeling she's going to try. Of course Guy is entitled to a lot more shares. Gerald virtually cheated him out of a large part of his inheritance."

"*What*?" Celine stared at her.

"Oh, it was legal enough, but after Lew died and Guy was still a boy, Gerald got up to all sorts of tricks to swing the balance of power. Muriel always *knew* but there was little she could do about it. You could say Gerald in being so generous to Guy has only cleared the slate."

"So that's why Guy never seemed surprised?"

"Good Lord, Celine," Helena said patiently. "Guy has grown up knowing what a rogue Gerald really was. There are no secrets between Guy and his grandmother. Both are determined a Harcourt will head Harcourt Langton. They don't trust the rest of us. Even Gerald regarded Guy as his natural successor. Clive spends his life trying to dominate people but he's not made of the right stuff. I'll have to move out to survive."

Celine sat down suddenly in the armchair beside the bed. "Seriously, Grandma?"

"I may look like a twit, I may even act like one, but believe me I'm not. There is no way I could live under the same roof as Clive and Imelda. I'm surprised they don't want to shove me into some discreet home."

"So what are we going to do?"

"I don't think we'll have to think long and hard. We'll have to move *out*!"

"Of course. That's understood." Celine nodded. "But where?"

"Get Guy to make inquiries about some property in the Never Never," Helena said with a strained smile. "It will take a miracle to move out *quietly*."

"They do happen!" Celine started up and moved towards a circular table covered with innumerable photographs in silver frames and a collection of Lalique birds. A crystal decanter stood atop it with a small gold-rimmed glass and Celine poured a small measure of the finest cognac into it. She walked back to the bed and handed the glass to her grandmother. "This will cause an uproar."

"Gerald should have thought of that," Helena said equably, taking a sip. "Clive might never speak to me again."

"I'm sure in his own way he would do his very best."

"One never knows. Does one?" Helena said. "In any case, I've never been able to swallow Imelda. Thank you, no. I must go my own way at long, long last. All I ask is you don't leave me until I'm properly on my feet. I have the feeling we'll have to weather a few storms."

"I'll go along with that," Celine replied with some feeling. "Why don't I find out what's on the market?"

Helena was silent for a bit, thinking. "What I'd really like is for Guy to design a house for me. A *small* house on one level. All I want is a view and a pretty surrounding garden. You can stay with me for as long as you like. But you're young with your life before you. You'll want a place of your own very likely. You'll marry." Her voice was suddenly very serious. "You won't find anyone better than Guy if you search the whole world."

"That's all over, Grandma."

"*Is* it?" Helena asked laconically. "It seems to me he's as protective of you as ever. I couldn't help noticing he held your hand in the library."

"I was shaking all over," Celine explained.

"Why should he care, if he's as bitter as you say?"

"That's a point, but Guy is a *gentleman* in the same way as his grandfather. Anyway he told me he's going to take over Harcourt Langton without any help from me."

Helena's expression said this was perfectly acceptable. "Good for him!" she remarked. "I'm not so old I don't find Guy tremendously exciting. Don't forget most of the money that started Harcourt Langton was put up by Lew. It was all tremendously sad, Guy losing his father, then his grandfather. People were always trying to marry Eloise off, but she never recovered, you know. Some women are like that. They care so deeply, no one else will do. Eloise made Guy her life. I expect she'll come into her own as a grandmother. I have to admit some of my grandchildren scare me. I was fascinated to see Michael making a big fuss of you before he left."

Celine frowned. "He actually kissed me on the mouth."

"He's always been attracted to you, Celine, but you never saw anyone else but Guy."

Celine looked and felt shocked. "Michael is my first cousin, Grandma."

"Different mothers." Helena shrugged. "Cousins marry. Especially when they want to keep a fortune in the family."

"This is weird!" Celine said, uncertain whether her grandmother was serious or not.

"No, it's life." Helena lay back against the pillows and closed her eyes. "Good night, my darling. A kiss before you go. Do you realise for the first time in fifty years I can no longer call my home my own?"

"I have a feeling, Grandma, it won't be a great loss," Celine said quietly. "What matters most is having a place of your *own*. A house that expresses *you*. Would you like me to speak to Guy or do you want to do that yourself?"

"No, you do it, darling," Helena responded tiredly. "At the moment I feel profoundly *lost*."

The voice on the telephone was almost as arrogant as that of her boss. "This is Ansley Forgan Smythe, Miss Langton," the woman announced herself. "Private secretary to Mr. Clive Langton. Mr. Langton wishes to set up an appointment to see you around threeish this afternoon."

Celine had her own ideas about that. She intended to spend the day with her grandmother. "I'm sorry, this afternoon isn't convenient," she said in her normal dulcet tones. "I could see my uncle the following morning, around elevenish," she added with the slightest hint of dryness.

The voice on the other end sounded enormously put-out. "Mr. Langton has a very tight schedule. I don't know..."

"I could make it ten-thirty if that would be helpful?" What the hell! It was useless trying to evade Uncle Clive.

Miss Forgan Smythe considered that and after a little cough finally agreed.

"What was all that about?" Helena asked after Celine had resumed her seat.

"Uncle Clive wants to see me."

"Of course he wants to see you," Helena said, calmly going about answering the sympathy cards she had kept apart. "He wants to know your plans. Most of them, anyway. I'd say he and Imelda are anxious to move in here. They might describe the place as a horror but it's big and imposing enough, even for them. Lew drew up such wonderful plans for a house, too. All kinds of lovely little surprises, especially for me. Gerald wouldn't have a bar of them. He never did have a good eye for architecture. He wanted a great fortress, someplace nobody could possibly overlook, not an elegant villa that opened out onto a beautiful garden. He had no spirituality, Gerald. Sometimes I feel I was tyrannised into an unhappy lifestyle. Of course I should have had some spunk, but I never learned how. Don't let that happen to you, Celine. Every woman has the right to her dream.''

Miss Forgan Smythe, a handsome, hard-faced woman, turned out to be one of those you're-up-against-a-stone-wall-type of secretaries. In fact it seemed to the gentle-mannered Celine, Miss Forgan Smythe was bent on giving her a hard time. She looked at Celine long and hard as though her one concern was establishing Celine *was* the person she claimed to be. Just as Celine was expecting to be asked for her driver's licence, Guy emerged from the executive floor lift.

"Celine!" He paused as he caught sight of her, then swung in her direction, so handsome and dynamic it was like the power had been switched on.

"How are you, Guy?" Unconsciously she lifted her face and he bent his raven head and brushed her cheek with the same lips that had once reduced her to mindless rapture.

"Fine." He turned to Miss Forgan Smythe, a slight frown on his face, as if asking for an explanation as to why Celine was standing. "What time is Miss Langton's appointment?"

"Ten-thirty, Mr. Harcourt." The secretary suddenly flushed.

Guy shot back an immaculate white cuff and looked at his watch. "Then you might like to buzz through to the office. It's ten-thirty now. I'm sure Mr. Langton wouldn't like to keep his niece waiting."

"Yes, of course, Mr. Harcourt." Miss Forgan Smythe took a deep breath then did as she was told, mouthing "I'm sorry" to Celine.

"May I talk to you when I'm through with Uncle Clive?" Celine asked Guy, while he was still exuding the old care for her.

"Of course. You know where to find me." He gave her a sardonic glance which clearly said "I'm not in the chairman's office. Not *yet!*"

Her uncle Clive was. He sat behind his late father's splendid desk, physically filling the space but lacking Sir Gerald's genuine *presence*. Light poured through the ceiling-high, plate-glass windows that afforded such a magnificent city and river scape but Celine was determined she wasn't going to sit in what she privately thought of as "the hot seat". The room brought back too many unhappy memories. It was the first time she'd been in it since that fateful day. It occurred to her now her grandfather had been an acknowledged business genius, but his private life had not been successful. Each member of the family had suffered in their own way. Had her grandfather been kinder or more understanding of a young woman's anxieties, who knows, things might have turned out quite differently for her. She mightn't have lost her chance at *her* dream.

"So, how are things at the house, Celine?" Clive Langton asked briskly, navigating his way through a pile of files as though she didn't warrant his undivided attention. "How's Mother? I can't seem to get through to her on the phone. Not your doing, I hope?" He glanced up accusingly, blue eyes afire.

"Absolutely not!" Celine spoke so crisply, his head, which had gone down again, snapped up. It had only taken Celine a couple of ticks to realise she had come a long way in a few years. She wasn't about to be browbeaten by her uncle Clive. "Grandma knows her *own* mind."

Clive actually snorted, then returned to the files again. "Then your knowledge of your grandmother is very small. Mother has never found making decisions easy. I've called you in here this morning, Celine, to confirm a few things. Your aunt Imelda is anxious to move into the house as soon as possible. She's a very impressive woman as I'm sure you agree. She's not overawed by the task of putting the house to rights. It's too startling, too much in Father's manner. There's much to be done and Imelda wants to make a start. If anyone can pull it off, she can. We assume you'll be looking for an apartment?"

"You may be *certain* of it, Uncle Clive," Celine said gently. "I haven't the slightest wish to inconvenience you or get tangled up in the alterations. Grandma and I were discussing it only this morning."

"Good. Good." Clive slapped a file shut with a decided thump. "I'm certain I could get you into Falcon Place. We built it, you know. You couldn't do better."

"Thank you, Uncle Clive, but we're thinking of a house." Celine touched a hand to her single strand of very fine pearls. Guy had given them to her for her eighteenth birthday. She thought of them as her magic charm.

"We? Who's *we*?" Clive rasped.

Celine lifted her soft grey eyes. "Grandma will want to talk to you herself, but she has authorised me to say she'll be wanting a place of her own."

Clive's heavy, handsome face turned crimson. "This is *your* doing, Celine. I'm not certain what's your motive."

Celine stared at her uncle thoughtfully. "You don't consider Grandma might want her independence?"

Clive almost choked. "My mother has had someone looking after her for *all* of her life. There is no way I would risk sending her out on her own. It would be a crime. Like having her committed. Father instructed me to look after her for the rest of her life. I take my responsibilities seriously, young lady."

"I know you do, Uncle Clive," Celine continued calmly, "but Grandma has reached a point in her life when she wants to make a new beginning."

Clive looked genuinely staggered. "Are you *mad*? Your grandmother is seventy-four. Not the most adventurous time of life, or so it seemed to me."

"A change can be great therapy, Uncle Clive. Grandma is showing courage. She is to be applauded. She's in good health. She's always taken care of herself. She could probably live another ten years or more. Like her own mother."

Clive looked as though he was losing control of what should have been a very minor exchange. "No matter what *Mother* wants, Father's wishes are paramount."

"Not anymore." Ruefully Celine shook her Titian head. "We all know Grandma endured a lifetime of benevolent oppression."

Clive's expression was ludicrous, a mixture of bafflement and anger. "You certainly *have* changed!" he accused her. "Only a few years ago you couldn't say boo to a goose. Ashley explains it as your need to assert yourself."

Celine smothered her hurt and sense of betrayal. "Don't listen to Ashley, Uncle Clive. She doesn't really know me at all. People change. They mature and grow. No matter how much we all loved and obeyed Grandfather it has to be said we all lived in fear of him. The truth fights to get out. Grandma feels the restraints of the past have been lifted from her. It's a kind of rebirth, if you like."

"What utter twaddle!" Clive gave a bitter laugh. "Old people do get these ideas. I'm telling you now, Celine, there's no way I'll condone Mother's setting up house. Especially not with *you*. Haven't you got enough without starting on your grandmother? Imelda intends doing up the east wing so Mother can have it all to herself. This is *no* time for her to be making decisions. She's in a state of shock."

"Then why don't you try to calm her?" Celine said in a reasonable tone. "As to what you mean by starting on her, I'm afraid I don't follow."

"Don't take that tone with me, young lady," Clive said, trying unsuccessfully to stare her down. "You've just about alienated all the family."

"That's no news, Uncle Clive. You didn't want me from the time I was born. You never offered any love or support to my father, much less my mother. I've never met with anything else but disapproval from you. As I recall, Aunt Imelda took violent objection to the way my hair curled. It's time now to make a stand. Don't make an enemy of me. You might regret it."

"Oh, my! Who would have thought you'd turn out a hothead!" Clive sneered.

"I think you'd better remember I'm Tiger Langton's granddaughter."

Silence. Best of all, a modicum of respect. "You'll never get close to Guy again, if you've got any plans there."

"Guy knows how to separate business from pleasure."

"You'll never get control. Either or both of you, so don't press too hard. Don't think I'm not awake to Guy. If he had his way he'd run every last Langton out."

"That might be the next step," Celine answered wryly, getting to her feet. "I won't take up any more of your time, Uncle Clive. When you do talk to Grandma I'd be very grateful for your understanding. If you love her you'll make it easy for her to move out."

"That I'll never do!" Clive thrust back his swivel chair so violently it crashed into the built-in cupboards. "Mother's future has been arranged. I am the head of the family now, Celine, and I'd thank you not to interfere."

Celine settled the gold chain on her handbag over her shoulder. "It's not interference, Uncle Clive, it's support. Grandma and I have spent enough time doing what we're told, as you're about to find out. I don't think it's too much to ask to be *listened* to. While I'm at it I should mention I'd like a job in the firm. We have a public relations department. I might do well there."

"Job? *Job*?" Clive Langton stared at her as if she'd taken leave of her senses. "My dear girl, you're an *heiress*!"

"Heiresses are people, aren't they? I'm used to working. I've spoken to my boss in Sydney. He understands I won't be able to return to my old job. I'm quite prepared to undertake further study, courses, whatever. I did very well at university though that was between me and the gatepost. Now that I think about it, only the Harcourts remarked on my intelligence."

"This is a very bad decision, Celine," Clive said, reaching for the heavy leather armchair and slumping down into it. "I'm very much against giving women power."

"So are most men your age, Uncle Clive. Hopefully you're a dying breed."

Guy's secretary showed her in; a striking young woman in her late twenties with long, gleaming, dark hair, clear green eyes and a charming manner. She also wore a diamond ring on her engagement finger, something that Celine noted with a sense of relief.

Guy rose immediately at her entry and came around the desk, settling a chair for her. "You look a little flushed."

"That's normal for an exchange with Uncle Clive." She smiled a little wanly.

"He does tend to raise the blood pressure," Guy offered suavely. "Would you like tea or coffee? If you're not due anywhere else I thought we might have an early lunch."

"That would be lovely! Yes to both." Celine slipped gracefully into the chair, crossing her slender legs at the ankles.

"Splendid!" he returned with mild mockery. He picked up the phone and murmured a few words into it, his eyes all the while moving lightly over Celine. She knew there was absolutely nothing about her that he missed. It wasn't exactly a glance of admiration, either. More a cool assessment. She was wearing her black Lagerfeld suit again as a mark of respect to her grandfather, but she had teamed it with a magnolia satin blouse almost the exact colour of her lustrous pearls. Her skin was an even richer cream, a flush of colour over her impeccable cheekbones, but she didn't see that. In any case for such a beautiful young woman Celine was curiously without vanity. Beauty she had found wasn't goodness or wisdom. Sometimes it could cause a good deal of distress.

Guy put the phone down, his expression turning faintly astringent. "Aren't they the pearls I gave you for your eighteenth birthday?"

She looked down and lightly touched them. "My lucky charm."

"Really?" One black eyebrow shot up.

"If you don't ask you'll never know."

"Then dare I ask if you're still wearing my ring?"

She hesitated only a moment, her flush deepening. "Have you any objection?"

"Maybe one or two. Possibly a dozen. I won't permit myself to dig deeper than that." He stood up abruptly and came around the desk. "I think I'm entitled to take another look at it. Ashley rather ruined the grand moment the last time."

Flustered Celine withdrew the beautiful ring that hung from its fine gold chain. She leaned forward a little and Guy took the weight of it in his palm. "I *do* remember it. Just hazily. The end of a fairy tale. The sleeping princess woke up and ran away and the prince turned into a frog."

"For what it's worth, I've always liked frogs."

He laughed at that. An uncomplicated sound and immensely attractive. Echoes of the old Guy who once would have caught her to him, dipping his head and finding her mouth.

"Yes, don't let's get caught up in all the old pain. Especially not since we're both big shareholders." He let his ring swing back against her breast and Celine tucked it up and slipped it through her blouse. "Grandma has decided to move out of the house. Me, too, of course."

"Great idea!" he said briskly, resuming his seat. "When do you want to go?"

"Uncle Clive is very much against it. In fact he was extremely angry when I told him."

"Domination is central to Clive's dealings. It's at the heart of just about everything he does."

"He could upset Grandma greatly," Celine said.

"It'll be Clive who has the heart attack. Nolan has the ulcers. Three at the last count. It has to be said Sir Gerald was responsible for a lot of that."

Celine nodded. "He never terrorised *you*."

"No. I'm a sucker for the *soft* touch. So far as Helena is concerned I'm at her disposal at any time. She would know that."

"She does. Sometimes I think Grandma is a little bit in love with you."

"Which makes her rather sharper than her grand-daughter. From now on I expect to be taken very seriously on the marriage market."

"You always were."

"You're kidding me, Celine." His black eyes gleamed. "So there's no woman in your life now?"

"I've absolutely no intention of telling you. Check with Ashley. I believe she does a brisk trade in gossip."

"I can promise you I don't listen to gossip," Celine said quietly.

"Oh, yes, you do, darling. After all, what happened to our engagement?"

"I was madly, gloriously in love with you, Guy." She lifted her mist-grey eyes.

"Ah, the halcyon days!" He locked his hands behind his elegant dark head and stared at the ceiling. "How sad they will never come again. The old Guy and his dewy Celine have quite disappeared. Maybe we *were* an odd couple."

He broke off as his secretary tapped on the door then entered carrying a tray.

"Thank you, Christine." He gave her a smile that was like being touched by sunlight.

"My pleasure!" She returned the smile with one of her own; one that might have set her fiancé brooding.

The coffee was exactly right and Celine sipped at it gratefully. If anything Guy's sexual radiance had increased. She felt the heat of it so exquisitely it was all she could do not to blow on her coffee.

"I take it Helena hasn't spoken to Clive yet," Guy asked, offering her a shortbread biscuit, which she refused.

"I don't think she can bear the weight of argument."

"So you need some help—right?"

"We can certainly use it. My own brief clash with Uncle Clive has confirmed that. What Grandma really wants is for you to design a house for her."

Guy stared at her thoughtfully. "I'd be delighted, of course. In fact I know just the site. It's a narrow block, part of the old McNally estate but it's high and cool with expansive views. The thing is, it would take a good six months to build and that's going flat out. The plans have to be drawn up and approved and we're looking at top-quality materials and workmanship."

"You can handle it, Guy."

"Of course I can. Where would you want to go in the meantime? The whole thing is already causing comment."

Celine lifted her eyes. "You mean about Grandma's not being left the house? How would anyone know?"

"Dear God, there are people out there who know more about Sir Gerald's will than you do. Besides, don't you think Clive and Imelda would find it a real pleasure to tell their friends they've inherited Langfield? It might have chimneys and towers and turrets popping up everywhere but some people think it's the ultimate stately pile. Imelda's probably been on the phone to the decorators already. If anyone wanted to know what was going to happen to Lady Langton they'd be told she would remain at Langfield where she'd be properly looked after."

Celine shook her head darkly. "Grandma doesn't need the benefit of their care. She wants to *own* her life. I don't blame her. It's a sad fact but Grandfather didn't listen to one word she said."

Guy smiled wryly. "No one is going to listen to you, Celine, if you first don't listen to yourself. Being put down has been a woman's lot for countless generations, but it's changing. Look at your own family. You and Helena have come on amazingly."

"A little miracle?" she challenged him.

"It's not so easy to tell now what goes on behind those luminous eyes."

"Yours are uncommonly fathomless, as well."

"So neither of us trusts the other. It sounds like you're planning on staying?" He gave her a cool, level glance.

Celine nodded. "I've already spoken to Max. He's disappointed but he knows it's not possible for me to go back to my old job."

"Such is life for an heiress!" Guy returned breezily.

"Don't *you* try to put me in a glass case."

"Terrific!" His handsome mouth turned down. "When did I *ever* do that? You are one cruel woman, Celine."

"I'd like to apologise. You never did that. It's important for me, Guy, to find something to do. In fact, I want a job at Harcourt Langton."

His black eyes sparkled with droll humour. "Darling, with a twenty percent share and a seat on the board you've *got* it!"

"I'm serious, Guy."

"So am I. Sort of. But I have enough conflicts to juggle without having you at the office. Doesn't it strike you as a kind of insanity?"

"I guess you're entitled to take these little swipes at me," she said.

"We were supposed to be madly in love, remember? Passionate stuff!"

"I didn't have the courage, Guy."

"Really? I thought you were waiting on a better offer."

"Obviously I didn't get it."

"Max was not your lover?" he asked in a hard, sceptical voice.

She lifted her mist-grey eyes. "You've mentioned this before."

"I'm mentioning it again. I enjoy asking questions."

"Believe that, you'll believe anything. Mel Gibson wouldn't have tempted me."

"Was *he* at the hotel? All right—" he held up a conciliatory hand "—let's establish what kind of work you'd like to do."

"Public relations," she said instantly. "I'd *have* to be better than Michael." She referred to her cousin.

"So who's arguing?" Guy shrugged.

"I saw him on television fielding questions about our proposed Manola Bay project."

"Your *uncle's* proposed Manola Bay project," Guy corrected. "They pushed it past the board but I'm not entirely happy about it. I've developed a reputation for my sensitivity to environmental problems. I want to stand by it. Keep the faith."

"I understand that, Guy." Celine was well acquainted with Guy's strong philosophies about architecture and the preeminence of nature. "Michael came out fighting as big business. What's worse is, he kept trying to put the woman environmentalist down. Even to the extent of talking over the top of her."

"Celine, I've seen it all before!" Guy said, an ironic expression on his face. "As it happens, it seems to run in your family. Michael can get nasty, but it's my opinion he thinks it's a way of impressing his father. Ridicule is a weak trick at the best of times. Clive wants Michael to take a higher profile in the firm. He's leaning on me to give Michael more responsibility but believe me he's not ready for it. In any case, Clive doesn't bring out the best in him.''

"Maybe he'd be better to get out of Harcourt Langton altogether?"

Guy nodded. ''He's at the point where he has to make a decision. The trouble is, and I never cease to marvel at it, Clive has him intimidated into the ground. Which is all the more remarkable he gave you that kiss. I didn't like it much. Did you?''

"Don't be an imbecile. Michael is my cousin."

"I *know*," Guy said bluntly. "Though what that might have to do with Michael's intentions... ?"

"Forget Michael." Celine waved her hands.

"I already have. So far as Manola Bay goes, Clive is really pushing the project and that means fast tracking it with the relevant government authorities. He seems to have the townspeople on side. The project would bring jobs, prosperity to the area, but until I have time to look at the environmental impact study I can't make an informed comment. I clash too much with Clive already and this is his baby. Dr. Bertram, the woman you're talking about, is a highly respected marine biologist. She's *not* one of the fanatical fringe. She knows what she's talking about. She must be listened to. There are many environmental issues we have to confront these days. It's a very sensitive area. I saw Michael myself. I can promise you I cringed. Both for him and for Harcourt Langton. Why he was the appointed spokesperson I'll never know. As you say, he's about as sensitive as a school of piranha. At the same time he made me think of a possible alternative site. A big parcel of land the firm bought many years ago. As I recall it was around four hundred acres with a couple of kilometres oceanfront. It's nowhere near as close to the Great Barrier Reef and there are no mangroves to consider. I have to wonder now why Clive and Nolan hit on Manola Bay.''

''I think *money* is the most important thing to them, Guy.''

''Sure. Catch anyone running a business where money's not important. But we're leaders in big property developments. We have to get things right for ourselves and the ones who follow us.''

''And P.R. plays a role.''

''Agreed,'' Guy said briskly. ''Let's discuss it over lunch.''

CHAPTER SIX

CELINE arrived home in a turmoil of feelings; excitement, elation, hope, a sense of challenge, as though the world was a different place. Lunch with Guy had been very successful, almost an unsettling replay of their former intense rapport. For sure they had both been a little on edge, more wary than unfriendly, but gradually they had relaxed, trading tales about how each had spent the past few years. At *work*, that is. Any hint of a personal life tended to bring out the acidity in Guy's vibrant tones.

It was all the more distressing then to have Mrs. Findlay rush at her the moment she stepped through the door.

"I'm so glad you're home, Miss Langton," she said, her competent face registering anxiety. "Mrs. Clive Langton is here with Ashley. They're with Lady Langton in the Garden Room."

"Thank you, Mrs. Findlay. I'll go through." Celine put her handbag down on a console table almost grotesquely decorated with ormolu and fat, gilded putti. Uncle Clive hadn't wasted any time! She glanced in the tall, gilded mirror that stood above the console, touching a hand to the radiant masses of her hair. This was going to be a test for herself and her grandmother. Curiously enough she had never been overbothered by her aunt Imelda, but as a shy and retiring schoolgirl she had often flinched at her cousin's sharp tongue.

Celine drew a deep breath as she entered the Garden Room with its high arched windows that led out onto an arcaded terrace. The room was bright with sunlight, wicker furniture and a wealth of tropical plants, golden canes, kentia palms, magnificent philodendrons and boston ferns, flowering orchids in great containers and hanging Tunisian birdcages filled with colourful begonias. All three women were seated at one of the circular, glass-topped tables. Ashley was nursing a drink in a tall, frosted glass, Imelda in a very natty navy-and-white outfit sat to the right of her, while Helena sat a little apart looking very much like a woman under siege. She needed bolstering and Celine regretted now she had spent a little time window shopping.

"You *do* look smart, Celine," Imelda said, somehow, as ever, implying disapproval. "One might even say *glowing*!"

"Having lunch with Guy obviously agreed with her." Ashley held up her glass to Celine in mock salute. "Guy's charm, when he bothers to turn it on, is legendary. *I* should know."

Why was Ashley such a puzzle? Celine thought. Why did she always sound faintly bitter when she was a young woman who had everything?

"Who told you I had lunch with Guy?" Celine asked casually, going to her grandmother, kissing her cheek then pulling up a chair beside her.

"Actually I spoke to him not ten minutes ago." Ashley's ice-blue eyes glinted.

"Really? And he told you we went out to lunch?" Celine could feel her heart racing but she willed herself to be cool.

Ashley let out a little, mocking laugh. "Guy and I are a lot closer than we used to be, Ceci."

Helena turned in her chair to stare at her elder granddaughter.

"What's so amazing about that, Gran?" Ashley asked in direct challenge. "Celine put herself very firmly out of the picture. I'm sure Guy would ask *me* to marry him if I'd only let him."

"Give it a try," Celine suggested briskly. "I don't like your chances."

"Sour grapes, kitten. It seems like *you're* trying for an encore. This time, I'm afraid, you'll have too much competition. Guy is a rare catch and he knows it. Ask him how many messages he gets on his answering machine." She reached out to stroke Celine's cheek, but Celine leaned away.

"No more about Guy. Not today. He may try hard to conceal his attraction to Ashley but a mother is never fooled. For now we have more pressing things to discuss," Imelda said sternly, turning in her chair to address Celine. "Your uncle tells me, Celine, you've been encouraging Mother to move out."

"He certainly didn't lose any time," Celine said wryly.

"Be that as it may, I've come to see if it's *true*!"

"I've already told you, Imelda, it's my own idea," Helena said in a voice cracking with irritation.

"Mother, you're in need of tender, loving care," Imelda told her in a firm voice. "You're under a great deal of stress."

Helena closed her eyes. "I've no doubt at all about that, Imelda, but I'm not as yet climbing up the walls. Celine is here now to minister to her poor, lame-brained grandmother, and Goldie and Mrs. Findlay wish to look after me, as well.''

That came as something of a shock to Imelda, who gasped. ''I assumed Mrs. Findlay went with the house?''

''Not at all, Imelda.'' Helena shrugged tiredly. ''She's a human being, not a piece of furniture.''

''You're distraught, Granny,'' Ashley said breezily, draining her glass.

Helena reacted with unaccustomed anger. ''I am not. Or I wasn't before you and your mother showed up. You drink far too much, Ashley. It's working against you.''

''How can you say that, Mother?'' Imelda bristled. ''It's only a gin and tonic.''

''And it's not yet three o'clock.''

''Oh, my!'' Ashley threw back her head and laughed, showing her beautiful teeth. ''What about all your Valiums, Granny? But that's okay.''

Imelda waved a quelling hand at her daughter. ''You must look at this properly, Mother,'' she argued, hunching forward and fixing her mother-in-law with a controlling glance. ''It's *far* too late in life to be thinking of starting up again. The house is *huge*! We can all live here quite happily without getting in one another's hair. I fully intend doing up the east wing for you.''

''Thank you, no, Imelda. I don't intend to be the skeleton in the cupboard. I'm not living in the east wing. It's so far away I'd have to fire off a rocket to get help.''

''Precisely!'' Celine burst out laughing at her grandmother's turn of phrase.

''Can't we be *sensible* about this?'' Ashley asked flatly.

''It doesn't really have anything to do with you, Ashley,'' Celine said in a reasonable voice. ''One great phase of Grandma's life has ended. She wants to take up the next. She *wants* a place of her *own*."

Imelda gave a clipped laugh and rapped on the glass-topped table. "My dear girl, Mother wouldn't know *how* to survive on her own."

"Please don't speak about me, Imelda, as though I'm not here," Helena implored. "I appreciate your concern on my behalf but you must allow me to go my own way. I don't want to bother anyone and *I* don't want to be bothered."

"Clive is totally against it," Imelda said as though that settled that. "He looks on it as a breach of trust. What would people think if we evicted you from your old home?"

"They'd think my marriage must have been a joke!" Helena responded, looking both sad and ironic. "Gerald should never have done this to me. The house would have passed to you and Clive in due time. As it *is*, I intend to start a new life. Even the lowliest senior citizen is entitled to an uprising."

Guy came up with a solution. *Fast*. He presented himself at Langfield that same evening, telling them David Forbes, the Q.C., and his wife, Pauline, were going overseas for an extended holiday. They would be only too pleased to let the house to Helena in their absence. It would be far more secure with a tenant, anyway, as David had pointed out. If Helena was interested they could discuss the matter further.

"Of course I'm interested," Helena said, suddenly looking brighter. "It's a lovely place. I've always liked it. I've been there many times, of course, both with

Gerald and on my own. Pauline is a tireless worker for charity. Do they know I intend to build?''

Guy nodded. ''I thought it best to tell them. They thought it quite exciting. I've secured the site, as well. The old McNally estate. Did Celine tell you?''

Helena looked fondly at her granddaughter. Tonight Celine was wearing a cool summer dress in the palest of pink and her beauty irresistibly drew the eye. ''Yes, she did. She told me *everything*. Oh, I'm so going to enjoy this!'' Colour touched her pale cheeks.

''If you're not entirely happy with the site, we can find another,'' Guy said. ''One day soon we'll have to go and look over it. It's a small block compared to what you're used to, roughly a quarter acre, but we can make it very private and containable. You won't want to be bothered with too much maintenance.''

''Perhaps we could take a run out there tomorrow?'' Helena suggested, then immediately looked embarrassed. ''You're far too busy, Guy. I don't know what I'm thinking of.''

''No problem, Lady Langton.''

''*Helena*, dear.''

''Helena.'' He gave her his charm-the-birds-out-of-the-trees smile. ''I have appointments all through the morning, but I'll be free in the afternoon. Shall we say, three o'clock?''

''We'll meet you there,'' Celine suggested helpfully. ''The sooner Grandma approves the site, the sooner you can start on the plans.''

''Helena seems a little happier in herself,'' Guy commented as Celine accompanied him to the door.

''Thanks to you. We had rather a bad afternoon.''

"Oh?" He paused to look down at her, his black eyes so brilliant and beautifully set they were enslaving.

"Aunt Imelda and Ashley turned up, as you surely know."

He drew away immediately, his expression tightening. "What is *that* supposed to mean?"

"Well, you did talk to Ashley," she was drawn into commenting, though she kept her tone quiet and matter-of-fact.

He continued to walk. "You have an *extraordinary* way of turning things around. Ashley rang *me*. I've no idea where from. She didn't say. I assumed she was at her own home."

"No, she was here with Aunt Imelda." Celine put on a little burst of pace and clutched at his arm. "I hope I haven't made you angry."

"Of course you've made me angry." He turned on her. "You're doomed to make me angry. When are you going to learn Ashley is an arch manipulator? Of the lot of you, she's the most like Sir Gerald."

"I recognise that, Guy." Celine stood in the full glare of the exterior lights, her hair a glorious cascade of colour. "She simply said . . ."

Guy gave a deep, goaded groan. "There's no *simply* anything with Ashley. She's very highly motivated. I wondered why the hell she rang me." He swung away towards the Jaguar parked in the shadows.

Celine went after him, her near-ankle-length skirt fluttering in the breeze that shook out all the scents of the garden. "Guy, it's none of my affair if you and Ashley have become friendly. I'm *glad*!"

"Oh, you're just too bloody sweet!" His voice was taut, pent-up. His anger hit her like a wave of heat.

"What do you want me to say?" She attempted to disguise her own inner turbulence but it clung to her like an aura.

"My lovely Celine, I refuse to be drawn into your net again. The last time almost destroyed me."

She couldn't bear to face to face the truth of that so she chose to deny it. "That's not true, Guy. There have been other women in your life."

He laughed bitterly. "I'm sure Ashley has given you a highly coloured account."

"What's with you and Ashley?" she implored. "You circle one another like a pair of tigers."

"I think you'll find it's claiming territorial rights," he told her harshly. "You carry compulsion about you, Celine. Ashley may be your cousin, but she's *not* your friend. She's possibly even dangerous."

"Oh, Guy!" Celine broke off in distress. "It's hard to accept that. I know Ashley isn't as straight with me as I thought she was. She's let me down. I've found that out, but she seems to be in some kind of pain herself."

"She can't get *everything* she wants," he explained bluntly. "I *must* go, Celine."

"Not on a note of anger. *Please*. We have to meet tomorrow. I'm so sorry if I've offended you."

"I'm sorry, too. I think you can judge your effect on me."

The wave of heat was now so extreme it was *sizzling*. She thought to kiss his cheek by way of apology, but as she swayed towards him he caught her about the waist, locking her to his lean, hard-muscled body.

"What is this, Celine? More of the heartbreaking magic? I've no intention of buying it."

"Guy, I've *known* you for most of my life."

"And you were, quite simply, the most beautiful little girl I've ever laid eyes on. The cherub I thought had escaped from your grandfather's painting. I should have known then you'd find a way to break my heart."

Conscience smote her. "Oh, Guy, I never meant it. I *swear*! It wasn't *you* I rejected. Never!" The words tumbled out in a kind of soft anguish. "Don't look at me like that."

"Like what?" he asked harshly. "With *desire*? Whatever I feel for you, Celine, that just won't die!"

With a burst of electric energy he grasped a handful of her hair, pinning her head back while he found her mouth. It was as if he still believed he had some claim on it.

It wasn't a gentle possession but dark and turbulent. There was even a flame of desperation in the sparkling violence. She heard herself moan, the merest little sound, but he didn't release her, neither was it over. He crushed her to him with a wilful passion, his mouth locked over hers, their tongues weaving and meeting in a strange mating dance.

Eventually he was driven to find her breast, cupping it with strong, thrilling fingers, the thumb moving sensuously back and forth over the nipple until it budded into a tight rose of sensation.

She was alive at last! The years rolled back. This was ecstasy, even if he was hurting her; an intoxication in the blood. She tried again to speak his name but he wouldn't let her. She could feel the *fierceness* moving through his body, the male power that was only just under control. Everything about him was so *perfect* to her, the contrast between his body and her own yet with the promise of becoming one flesh. She savoured the scent and texture of his skin, the feel of his fine, long-fingered hands as he *electrified* her smooth skin. Sensation was too exquisitely excruciating to speak of caresses.

Just as her admission of love was being forced out of her, he drew back abruptly, making it perfectly clear to her who had the upper hand. The whole dazzling incident had only taken a few moments but she was trembling so badly she might have passed through the eye of a storm.

The night breeze blew, shaking out a cascade of blossom from the jacaranda above them. He still held her with one arm, while she stared up at him dazedly, her hair a wild cloud around her oh-so-aroused face.

"You've kissed me like that only once before."

His chiselled features seemed more tightly etched. "Like then, you drove me to frenzy. Passion has the power to overwhelm the mind. I could make love to you until you ached and burned all over. You're perfectly designed for obsession, but then I remember how it was. The pain and the loss of meaning in my life. The realisation you'd fled me as someone you couldn't trust with your life and your love. Of course you could tell me that's my male ego. Maybe it is. All I know is, I'll never lose control of my life again."

Tears shimmered in Celine's luminous eyes. "So you *hate* me. You really do." She didn't think she could bear it.

"God help me, Celine, I could never hate you." He turned away and opened the door of his car. "Only this time, it's *your* turn to pay."

*   *   *

After that many things happened quickly. Helena approved the site for her new home, emerging as a woman who could make on-the-spot decisions virtually overnight. No one would have thought it possible, but it was. It was as though Helena had rediscovered the identity she had long considered lost. It staggered the rest of the family who reacted as though they had confidently expected her to go into a very serious decline.

"I don't understand it myself," Helena confided to Celine in private. "Maybe it's a last burst of the human spirit. Of course, you're here to add your invaluable support and Guy's always good for real muscle. Clive thinks shouting is what it's all about. He's more concerned with what people will think rather than my well-being."

On the day they shifted out of Langfield, Guy was there to prevent a cheerless departure. Clive and Imelda stood on the front steps loudly bemoaning the fact Helena had chosen to make a "public spectacle of them". Ashley, too, was on hand to help stir the pot, demanding Guy call her just as they were driving off.

"Why don't you get an unlisted number, Guy?" Helena suggested. "Ashley's trying just too hard to be clever."

With her grandmother comfortably installed at the Forbes estate, Celine flew off to Sydney to finalise her own affairs. On the last evening she managed to find time to have a pleasant dinner with Max. Max was in high spirits, confiding there was a new woman in his life, a well-known interior designer in charge of current refurbishment at the hotel.

"Third time lucky!" he quipped.

It would *have* to be if one learned anything, Celine thought, but sincerely wished him well.

A few days after she returned home she was required to attend her first board meeting. It was heady stuff for a twenty-three-year-old. She felt a huge wave of anticipation. Over the past years she had become aware she was of one life's workers. She enjoyed being kept busy, meeting new challenges. She wanted to succeed in life, not as Tiger Langton's granddaughter, but on her own terms. She wanted her life to have some real meaning. It had always seemed very strange to her Ashley had chosen to frolic her life away. Even Aunt Imelda was seriously into charity work.

On the morning she was due in the city she went looking for her grandmother to get her opinion. "So, what do you think, Grandma?" she asked, holding a pose.

Helena put down her newspaper, bending a professional eye on her grand-daughter. "Peachy!"

"Gosh, then I haven't pulled it off. I was going for a touch of power dressing."

Helena made a small scoffing noise. "You're too feminine for that. The suit is lovely. Tailored, yes, but *soft*. The short skirt shows off your dancer's legs. Years ago redheads were supposed to avoid pinks like the plague. Fancy that! All shades of pink suit you beautifully."

"Wish me luck, Granny." Celine bent and kissed the top of her grandmother's head.

"I do, my darling. Don't expect your uncles to clasp you to their manly bosoms. At least you'll have Guy and Muriel. The rest of them will succumb to your beauty but they won't think you'll have anything to contribute. You'll have to change that, Celine.''

"I'm going to try, Grandma.'' Celine picked up her bag, settling the long gold chain over her shoulder.

"And I applaud it. My life would have been very different had I realised my own worth instead of accepting Gerald's one-eyed views. Who knows, in time, you might be capable of running the corporation.''

"Guy might have something to say about that,'' Celine pointed out in a dry voice.

Helena waved an airy hand. "Then run it together.''

The atmosphere of the boardroom embraced her the moment she walked in. It actually smelled of big business and decision-making. The room was spacious, mahogany-panelled with a coffered ceiling and Biedermeier-inspired furnishings which included the thirty-foot-long boardroom table and the surrounding chairs. Guy was holding the floor, a group of board members assembled around him. Her uncles were seated heads together at the table, deep in discussion. Near the tall windows Lady Harcourt was laughing at something Sir Peter Hartford, retired banker and long-time board member, was saying.

All heads swivelled at her entrance. Guy looked towards Clive, naturally expecting him as chairman to be the first to go forward to welcome his niece, but when Clive continued to remain seated, fidgeting with some papers he had before him, Guy lost no time crossing the room.

"Welcome to your first board meeting, Celine.'' He took the hand she extended. "You look like a peach tree in blossom.''

"Should I have worn something more conservative?" she asked seriously.

"Not at all. We men get enough of that. Now, come and meet everyone. Some you already know. Not Nancy, she's new...Ian Prentice, he has a seat on a dozen boards..."

Within moments Celine was surrounded, exchanging greetings or introductions. Lady Harcourt and Nancy Rawlings were particularly pleasant to her and it wasn't long before they took their appointed seats at the big, gleaming table. The meeting began, the first business of the morning to officially welcome Celine to the board and confirm her non-executive directorship.

While the meeting was in progress Celine's face was a study in concentration. She had so much to learn! Public relations, dealing with *people* was a far cry from mind-boggling figures, financial reports, working hours, targets, suppliers, politics. When Guy spoke, which was often, he had everyone's total attention, including, Celine noted, her uncles'. Most of the men in the room were a good twenty years and more his senior, yet it was quite obvious they looked on him as their equal when it came to business; maybe in a few cases, distinctly their superior. Guy had such a mastery of his subject, of "common sense business principles" as Sir Gerald had used to call them, he was now at the top of his profession and still in his early thirties. Obviously the sky was the limit, Celine thought, which meant becoming chairman of Harcourt Langton. It was hard to look away from him. His voice and manner though always completely composed had such *authority* she had no difficulty seeing him as her grandfather's legitimate heir.

The packed agenda was drawing to a close when Guy brought up the subject of the Manola Bay project. He stood up from the table, went to a cabinet and picked up a pile of folders which he proceeded to distribute around the table.

"These are copies of the environmental impact study," he explained as the members began to open them up. "They weren't available up until now."

Clive's face flushed crimson. "Are you saying I've been withholding them?"

"*You* said that, Clive," Guy answered calmly.

"So where did you get it from?" Nolan, too, was red in the face.

"I have my sources, Nolan." The faintest of smiles touched Guy's cleanly-cut lips. "I know you were going to bring it to our attention. I've managed to do it a little earlier."

"Do you have something to tell us, Guy?" Sir Peter asked, his expression indicating he wanted to hear.

Guy resumed his seat. "First of all I'd like you all to read the report. I'll tell you now I'm opposed to the project in its present form. In my opinion, the whole development has to be scaled back. More safeguards have to be worked in. Especially in relation to waterways."

He continued to talk for about ten minutes with the confidence of the expert. Clive scowled and scowled but didn't interrupt. Nolan doodled frenetically. Guy concluded by saying he was confident if the project was pulled back to a more manageable scale and the measures he'd outlined adopted, they would win the support of the strong environmentalist lobby which now opposed the project. He then went on to draw the board's attention to a possible alternative site for the larger scale development.

"Cape Clarence, if anyone remembers. We bought it years ago. As far as I can recall some four hundred acres with a two kilometre oceanfront. Sir Gerald said at the time it was the ideal site for future tourist and residential resort development. I haven't as yet had the time to look it up, but the Manola Bay project jogged my memory."

"Ah, yes!" Sir Peter and one or two others began to recall the acquisition by the firm.

When Celine glanced up at her uncle she was alarmed to see the florid colour had drained right out of his face. "What is it, Uncle Clive?" She stood up automatically. "Aren't you well?"

Clive, in a slumped position, jerked upright. "Of course I'm well," he said icily.

"You certainly don't look it," Lady Muriel intervened, a certain reproof in her tone.

"I'm really not in need of your concern, Muriel."

"You're sure of that?" Lady Muriel asked on a dry note of challenge.

Nolan jumped up as if he meant to restrain his brother. "Perhaps we can bring the meeting to a close? This is our first meeting without Father. Naturally Clive and I are feeling it."

"Shouldn't we include Celine?"

"Of course, Celine," Nolan said hurriedly, not meeting Lady Muriel's fine, dark eyes.

Guy took charge. "That's okay with me." He looked around at the other board members who unanimously nodded their heads. So the meeting was concluded with the Manola Bay project still up in the air.

"What was that all about?" Celine overheard Lady Muriel ask of her grandson. Everyone had begun to disperse in a flurry of goodbyes.

"Something gave Clive *and* Nolan a nasty shock!" Guy's brilliant, black eyes were narrowed, as though trying to fathom what it was. "It seemed to coincide with the mention of the Cape Clarence site."

"You'd better look into it," Lady Muriel advised. "You don't suppose they could have possibly sold it off?"

"Not unless they were mad, and they're not! That land today would be worth a fortune."

"Perhaps Clive was just furious with you for undermining his pet project. Be *careful*, darling. You have an enemy there."

"Really? I never noticed." Guy gave a brief, ironic smile. "So where are you off to?"

"A luncheon in honour of Maggie Hoffman." Lady Muriel mentioned a well-known woman politician. "She's really a wonder! She has the respect of both sides of the house."

At this point Celine wandered over to say her own goodbyes.

"Lots to learn, Celine?" Lady Muriel smiled at her.

"So much! Did Guy tell you I wanted a job?"

Lady Muriel nodded. "Good for you, Celine. You have all you need to succeed. So when are you coming to have dinner with us? I'd ask Helena, of course, but she tells me she's not going out for a while. I have to say she sounded a whole lot better."

"She is, in a number of ways. Would Wednesday be too soon?"

"Wednesday would be fine. Shall we ask Guy to come?"

Was Lady Muriel trying to reconcile them? "He might say no."

Guy's answer was a fraction slow. Like a man put on the spot and too gracious to decline. "Not if Gran serves a good old-fashioned lamb roast," he managed smoothly.

"I'll be happy to see Maybelle does. Shall we say 7:00 p.m? Guy, you'll pick Celine up?"

"Whatever you say, Gran." He gave her a challenging stare not unlike her own. "If you've got some time tomorrow, Celine, I'd like to show you around the various departments. There have been lots of changes. I understand you can't start work immediately, but you can get to meet the staff."

"Not Miss Forgan Smythe." Celine smiled wryly. "I've already had the pleasure."

"Why don't we all pray for her to find a husband," Lady Muriel said.

CHAPTER SEVEN

WHEN Celine presented herself at the executive suite of offices, "the hub of the empire" as her grandfather had used to call them, all very grand and beautifully furnished, she found Guy in a decidedly crisp and businesslike mood. He rose with a smile that showed his beautiful, white teeth but the smile didn't reach the intense dark of his eyes. She felt it in her head and in her heart. Life was very much a shuffle, she thought. One step forward, two steps back. Nevertheless he took her on the grand tour, stopping in each department to introduce her to key personnel and occasionally the lowliest on the chain. Harcourt Langton employed architects, engineers, draughtsmen, surveyors, lawyers, accountants, administrators and their own public relations people.

Michael Langton, who had not shone academically but had been exceptionally good on the sports field, had been dumped in that department. As they reached his big, corner office, he jumped up from behind the desk and came around, grasping Celine's arms and kissing her yet again a bare inch from her mouth. Celine just stopped herself from wiping it off, something that was lost on Michael. He gestured them into chairs, sitting back on his desk, arms folded, his thickly lashed blue eyes sparkling with uncousinly admiration. Over the past few years he had filled out and Celine realised he would

106

look *exactly* like his father in time. He was blond, handsome, sensual in the way Ashley was sensual.

"This is going to be *fun*, Ceci, having you on the premises."

"Fun? I don't think so, Michael," Guy said.

"I'm hoping to fill my time with work, Michael," Celine added with a pleasant smile.

"Really?" He looked amazed. "Some days I go potty looking for something to do."

"I'm sure we can fix that," Guy commented, looking deadly serious.

"Just joking, Guy." Michael grinned. His eyes travelled down Celine's slender body in a citrus yellow silk dress to her legs and elegantly shod feet.

Whatever Celine had expected, she hadn't expected this. In fact, she felt an element of shock. She remembered the time she had played the piano at the Beaumont when some of the men had looked at her as if she were a peach to be plucked. She didn't expect it of her cousin, but it was happening right in front of her eyes. Ashley had told her all the girls in Michael's department were madly in love with him, but there was something about him she found distinctly off-putting. Guy must have thought so, too, because his tall, lean body moved restively.

"Would you like me to show you around?" Michael suggested, sounding expansive. He was, after all, the chairman's son.

"We did stop to speak to a few people on the way in," Guy returned, slightly repressively.

"Good, good!" Michael boomed, reminiscent of his father. "So where are we going to put Ceci? There's room enough in here. I don't mind sharing. Quite the reverse!"

"You're too nice, Michael," Guy said in his smoothest voice. "We can fix Celine up with an office of her own."

"Not too far away. I get lonely," Michael said. "Let's do lunch one day, Ceci. I haven't had a chance to talk to you properly since you got back."

"Fine, Michael. I'll give you a call when I'm available."

"Still tickle the ivories?" he asked.

"That's certainly a cute way of putting it," Guy said.

"I don't practise as much as I should," Celine intervened without missing a beat.

"That must have been one hell of a job playing at that piano bar?" Michael grinned. "Gramps was *livid*! There are too many crazies running around out there. You're one beautiful girl!"

Celine felt a sharp stab of irritation. "I managed to survive. The Beaumont is a five-star hotel, Michael. I was well looked after. The job was short-lived in any case. I spent nearly all my time in P.R."

Something faintly malicious crept into Michael's bright, smiling expression. "It must have been tough on you leaving your boss. Wasn't there just a hint of romance?"

"No, Michael." Celine denied it gently, refusing to take the bait. She could have added Max was shortly to remarry but didn't think it was any of Michael's business.

"That's not the way I heard it!" Michael crowed, sounding much like Ashley. "I heard he came on pretty strong. A real womaniser!"

"Obviously a wild story," Guy said in a curt voice, and stood up, glancing at Celine in an indication she should do the same.

"Or that's all you're going to tell us, eh, Ceci?" Michael persisted. "You've lost a lot of that head-in-the-clouds, little-angel look. Why, you're downright sexy!"

"Surely that's an inappropriate remark?" Guy asked abruptly.

"Well, she *is*, Guy. Extremely sexy."

Something changed in Guy's face. Enough to give Michael pause. "You've made your point."

"Ceci knows I mean no offence."

"I really should be getting back to Grandma," Celine said, more to end a bad moment than anything else. "Apart from which, Guy, I'm taking up your valuable time."

"So how's dear old Gran?" Michael asked at once, not bothering to wait for an answer. "Say hello to her for me. Better yet I'll come over soon for a nice long chat."

"I'd wait a while, Michael," Celine advised. "Grandma is taking things very quietly at the present time."

"You're pulling my leg!" Michael rolled his eyes heavenwards. "Gran's escapades have set the whole town on its ears. Mum and Dad think she's gone bonkers!"

"Perhaps they like to look on the negative side of things," Guy said shortly. "No, I have an urgent appointment in about half an hour. We'd better go back upstairs, Celine."

"Take care of yourself, Ceci!" Michael called. "It's going to be a real pleasure having you around the place."

"To my way of thinking Michael ought to be turfed out of Harcourt Langton," Guy said, turning to face

Celine at the lift. "All he's ever had going for him is muscles!"

Celine groaned. "Why on earth is he making a play for me?"

"It's called common lust," he told her bluntly.

"Thank you. Now I know."

They stepped into the lift, which was mercifully empty.

"I presume you want to stay with P.R.?" Guy asked, looking stern.

"You think Michael might be a problem?"

"I think you could handle it but you'd have to have an endless reserve of patience. It might be an idea if you spend time in each department in turn."

"Whatever you think, Guy. Ashley told me all the girls in Michael's department are in love with him."

Guy gave a laugh just the least bit menacing. "They've got better taste."

In his office he handed her a medium-sized padded bag, the kind issued by all post offices.

"What's this?" She looked down at it, noting it was addressed to Guy at the Harcourt Langton building, not the private box. "I'm supposed to open it?"

"It's of you, after all!"

"All right," she said faintly, disturbed by his tone. "What a one you are for mysteries!"

"What a one you are for deceptions."

"I don't buy that. Not at all." She drew out a couple of glossy photographs, staring down at them blankly. "What the heck is going on?"

"Something I might ask you."

She looked up into his brilliant black eyes. "Who took these and why would they send them to you?"

"Certainly not for the stamps," he said at his most sarcastic. "I suppose *some* people might think I still care."

"This is *wrong*!"

"You mean, there are *more*?"

"Please, Guy, I know nothing about this." Celine stared down at the photograph on top. It was an excellent one and she didn't stop to think she looked lovely. It showed her bent over Max, both hands clasped on his shoulders, hair cascading while she kissed his cheek. Max had his head thrown back, obviously enjoying it immensely. The second photograph showed them staring at one another soulfully, hands interlocked. To anyone who didn't know the situation it might have appeared they were lovers. Max was years older, overweight, but even the photographs revealed he was a man who was extremely attractive to women.

"This was taken the last night I was in Sydney," she tried to explain.

"I guessed that. It must have been a very pleasant dinner indeed."

"It was delightful!" Celine stared at him.

"My own feeling is he's too old for you and he's starting to go to fat."

Celine shook her head. "He looks heavier in the photographs. Guy, there's something I must tell you."

"*Don't. Please!*" He came around the side of his desk, wearing his most cynical expression. "I'm on my way. I told you I had an urgent appointment."

"This will only take a moment." She gripped his jacketed arm. "Max is remarrying."

"Of *course* he is!" Little brackets of scorn etched themselves into the sides of his beautiful mouth. "And you're the lucky woman?"

"Not at all!" She blinked. "Holly Lewis is."

"And who the hell is she?" he asked pleasantly.

Celine was amazed. "You *don't* know Holly Lewis?"

"That's right!" He sounded testy. "Is she a well-known person?"

"Why, she's possibly the finest interior decorator in the country."

Guy stared at her a moment longer, then he passed a hand across his eyes. "*That* Holly Lewis?"

"I was surprised when you said you didn't know her. It's a wonder you haven't met her at some time."

"I think I have." Guy unceremoniously dumped his disclaimer. "You're telling me Max Kenton is marrying Holly Lewis?"

"Isn't it splendid!" Celine's grey eyes lit up. "The moment Max told me I swooped on him with a kiss."

"I can't help thinking he didn't deserve the degree of ardour, but all right, I accept that."

Celine laughed for the first time, a sweet, engaging sound. "So you *should*! Naturally I'd enjoy your apology."

"You're going to get it!"

His movements were so swift and supple, so masterful in their intent, Celine had the sensation of losing her balance. She clutched at him while his hand encircled her chin. "Your mouth is the colour of watermelon," he murmured hypnotically, his thumb moving up to slide over it.

"You used to love it." Her heart shook with a desperate passion.

"So I did!" Time seemed to stop. He bent his head and took possession of her mouth in a kiss so brief, yet so deep and urgent, her body *flowed* towards his.

Oh, God, Celine thought. *I love you... love you... love you.*

"Remember where you are, Celine," he admonished her, his warm breath mingling with hers.

"You started this," she whispered. It was true his kiss had left her feeling so vulnerable she didn't quite know where she was.

"And I'm not following it up with a marriage proposal." He kissed her very quickly again, determined to make light of it.

"I don't expect you to." The expression in her misty grey eyes was as soft as a peace offering.

"I've been burned once. Twice is too much!"

"That sounds fair to me." She followed him a little breathlessly to the door. "Do you intend to remain a bachelor?"

He made another of those lightning turns. "Not unless I can't catch myself a rich dolly bird."

"But you're rich yourself."

"Well, not to *excess*! In any case, I'm talking nonsense. Come along, Celine. Business calls."

It was only as she was driving home Celine began to ponder in earnest who might have sent the photographs. Clearly they were intended to muddy her image in some way, so they were personal. She hadn't told a soul she was having dinner with Max at the hotel. Correction, she had told her grandmother when she had rung home during the day, but her grandmother was the last person in the world to have any involvement in such a sad little ploy. The photographs were the glossy variety taken by a professional. Was it possible, now she was a minor celebrity, she would be prey to this kind of thing? No one could deny it happened. But why send the photographs to Guy? That was as good a lead as anything to the sender's motive and identity.

Irresistibly she thought of Ashley. Ashley had a rather peculiar sense of humour. Neither was she to be trusted. She had learned that the hard way. But how could Ashley have known, let alone have found the time to set it up? She was being naive. All it would take was money and a phone call. She gave a little shiver of distaste. It wasn't nice to know she was the object of someone's malice.

Celine spent a quiet but rewarding fortnight keeping her grandmother company. Then on Helena's insistence she started work, not as an executive or anything like it, more an apprentice in training. Clive had told her from the beginning he was against the move, but Nolan greeted her the first morning albeit with no obvious sign of pleasure. Guy on the other hand told her he was delighted she intended to take her training seriously, then immediately threw her in the deep end, clearly expecting her to survive.

She was to spend a few months in each department in turn. If she'd hoped or expected to start with the glamour department, architecture, she was doomed to disappointment. The very first morning she went into accounting, where she was greeted in friendly fashion with no hint of deference. That suited Celine fine. She wanted to be treated just like any other employee. After the first week it was apparent her wish had been granted in spades.

She was swamped in the humdrum, but no one ever heard her complain. In fact she won some admiration for her cheerfulness and level of commitment. She sensed one of the girls was vaguely hostile to her, but she couldn't think why and she didn't dwell on it. She waded through mountains of invoices, checking and entering into the computer, which sometimes gave her a headache. She reconciled accounts, fielded telephone enquiries and took photocopies. In short, she did everything that was asked of her.

The only real problem was Michael. He took to lying in wait for her, or more embarrassingly, coming down to the accounts department pestering her for a lunch date. Finally to get it over, Celine gave in. On the particular Friday she was combing her hair and touching up her lipstick in the rest room when the hostile girl, Marcy, followed her in.

"So where are you off to?" she asked with more than a hint of challenge. She had oddly coloured eyes, one brown, one greenish brown.

"A lunch appointment," said Celine pleasantly, leaning towards the mirror, lipstick pencil in hand.

"With Michael?"

"As it happens. Why?" Celine was aware her voice had cooled.

The strange eyes flashed. "No need to get off your high horse. Michael and I had a thing going at one time. Surely he told you? Of course I knew it wasn't going anywhere. The rich stick to their own when it comes to marriage."

Celine turned, giving the other young woman her full attention. "Was it as serious as that?" Marcy was very attractive in her fashion. Olive-skinned, brunette, her eyes set at a provocative slant. Now she looked as though she was fighting hard to hold in her jealousy and resentment.

"No, it *wasn't*. Michael was always out of reach, but he knew where to take his pleasure."

So that explained the odd hostility, Celine thought. She put her lipstick back in her bag and shut it. "I'm sorry you've been hurt, Marcy, but this isn't any of my business."

"I thought it might be since Guy Harcourt slipped your net. You've turned our attention to Michael. He *is* one sexy hunk!"

"He's also my cousin. *Family*."

"That's not the sort of vibes I'm getting."

"I have to tell you, Marcy, I don't care." The sooner I get out of here the better, Celine thought.

"Do you mind if I ask you a question?" Marcy persisted, following her to the door.

I must be crazy, Celine thought, but she relented. "Get on with it."

"My God, you must know how I feel!" Marcy cried emotionally. "There's *your* ex-fiancé romancing your cousin, Ashley."

There was a moment Celine thought all the blood had pumped away from her heart, leaving her icy cold and bereft. "I wasn't aware he was." She was astounded her voice remained calm.

"He *is*, dear." Marcy snorted. "Unlike *you*, apparently, I know a lot about it. Michael would tell me everything in bed. Besides, I caught them together in the executive lift of all places."

"Surely you shouldn't have been there," Celine retorted, sounding for the first time like the Langton heiress. "In any case, both of them are free agents. Why *exactly* are you telling me all this? You obviously aren't in any way kindly disposed to me."

"Maybe I'm more on your side than you think. Both of us, *losers*," Marcy explained. "If you're not romantically interested in Michael and I have to say you sound convincing, I have to warn you he's one persistent guy. He keeps at it and at it until he gets what he wants. The *chase* is everything with Michael. Once he's got you he very quickly tires."

"I'll be sure to remember." Celine was fighting hard to keep her composure. She put her hand on the doorknob.

"Don't let me stop you," Marcy called. "You wouldn't want to keep cousin Michael waiting."

The maître d' showed them to their table, one of the best in the riverside restaurant. Though Celine kept her eyes trained ahead, she couldn't help but be conscious of the interested gazes all around her. In fact the hum of chatter had abruptly subsided the moment they walked in. Langton was a prominent name in the city and as such the family was used to attracting curious and often envious eyes. Michael had her rather possessively by the elbow, shepherding her through the tables while continuing to wave expansively here and there. It was now well into November so Celine had dressed for the heat in finest white linen. The purely simple dress was oval-necked and sleeveless but she had added a wide belt worked with azure, emerald and turquoise adornments. Her handbag matched and she had strappy high-heeled sandals on her feet. Michael, with the build of a fullback, wore an expensive summer-weight suit in an attractive caramel shade and she realised they must have made an eye-catching couple. There was no family resemblance between them. She had inherited her grandfather's brilliant red-gold hair but her features and her light-limbed frame were inherited from her mother. Michael was all Langton, big, blond and handsome with the Langton ice-blue eyes. No one would have taken them for first cousins.

As soon as they were seated Michael ordered a bottle of chardonnay even though Celine shook her head. She had no intention of drinking in the middle of the day. In any case she had to go back to work. Mind and body in disarray, she gazed out the window at the river; deep and wide, a paddleboat was wending its way upstream, its decks filled with tourists and patrons who delighted in a long, leisurely seafood lunch. On the opposite bank, one of the oldest parts of the city, the great spreading poincianas were breaking out into sumptuous orange-red blossom, the radiant colour enhanced by the bright green of the delicately leafed fronds and the intense blue of the sky. *Everything*, the water, the trees, the paddleboat and the old white-washed buildings shimmered in the soft luminosity of the heat haze. It was a lovely, relaxing scene, but no way Celine could enjoy it. Could it *possibly* be true? Guy and Ashley? Michael would know, but she knew she could never bring herself to ask him.

"You're a little pale, Ceci," Michael said, blue eyes skimming over her face and breast. "Not that I don't adore your skin. It's like a baby's. Poreless, flawless. Makes you want to touch it." He picked up the menu. "Now, what are you going to have? We've got all afternoon."

"No we *haven't*. Michael," Celine roused herself to say emphatically, "I have to get back to work."

"You're joking, sweetie!" Michael scoffed.

"I'm not laughing. I'm working, Michael. Not playing at it. I just have the hour."

"Don't be absurd!" Michael looked at her narrowly, reminding Celine vividly of his sister Ashley. He leaned across the table, speaking confidentially. "What are you playing at, Ceci? Here you are looking like a dream and you're talking about going back to work. *Accounts*, for God's sake! If I didn't know you were so intelligent I'd say you needed your head read."

"Then there's nothing more to be said. I'll go now." Celine began to gather up her handbag and sunglasses.

"Ceci, sweetie! Have a care!" Michael very quickly put his hand over hers. "Just about everyone in the restaurant is staring at us. If you're serious, all right. I just didn't think you would be. Don't let's spoil what time we have."

Celine just had to speak; to put the developing situation right.

"Michael, forgive me if it's out of order, but you're speaking as though we're on a *date*!"

"Aren't we?" Michael looked at her strangely. "I've always been attracted to you, Ceci. At the same time I've always been afraid of Guy."

Celine considered that in amazement. "Afraid of Guy? Guy isn't the sort of person to inspire fear. Admiration, respect, hero worship, if you like, but not fear. Grandfather was the one to do that."

"Let me put it another way," Michael said, staring at her. "I've always been in some awe of Guy. He may not be forbidding or anything like that—he has too much charm—but he's very formidable when he has to be.

Guy's going to end up chairman of Harcourt Langton, don't you worry. It's going to kill Dad but it's going to happen. Sooner rather than later. Just between the two of us, Guy's our man. He's in another league from Dad. Why do you think Gramps gave him so much power? Even with Dad interim chairman, Guy is the real boss. Look how he got his way over the Manola Bay project.''

"He did, but we all voted on it. What has this got to do with *us*, Michael?''

Michael started to trace patterns on the salmon-pink tablecloth. "You always belonged to Guy. I swear he fell in love with you when you were six years old. You captivated him then. The thing is, I fell in love with you, as well, only I didn't know it at the time. You were the very opposite of Ashley. You were always so sweet and sympathetic and gentle. Just to be with you was to stop hurting. Ashley's my sister and I guess I love her. I know I'm supposed to, but she's very intolerant. She would never permit me to be her friend. I was always dumb, or a nuisance. You were her little pet. She loved you.''

"She doesn't now?'' Celine asked with a saddened expression.

"You've grown up, Ceci. You don't run to Ashley anymore for comfort. You're a lot of things she isn't and it stings her to the quick. Besides, you're in competition.''

"How? Ashley wants no part of Harcourt Langton.''

"I mean *Guy*!'' Michael groaned. "God, Ceci, she's mad for him. Surely you know?''

"Things might have been different if I had. I thought they were incompatible. No love lost between them.''

"That's just Ashley's way,'' Michael assured her. "She's always wanted Guy and why not? Who the hell else is like him? The tragedy was he wanted you. Ashley had to accept it. These days it's a different matter. Guy didn't take being jilted too kindly. Frankly I don't think he'll ever forgive you. They're all being very polite, the Harcourts are like that, but I can tell you they were devastated for Guy. Why *did* you do it, Ceci? I would have thought the two of you meshed perfectly, like two pieces in a puzzle."

"I thought I wasn't woman enough for him, Michael."

"I don't believe it."

"It's true."

"Well you've lost him, sweetie," Michael said gently. "Ashley told me, not that I can accept every word she says, she's inclined to be a little careless with the truth, the two of them have been playing at a silly love-hate. That's apparently over. I suppose it's quite possible even while he loved you he was attracted to her. She's supposed to be very sexy."

"She is as *you* are, Michael, but I have to tell you I look on you as *family*."

"Well, I hope to change that, Ceci," Michael said with a faint swagger. "There's no impediment to any relationship between us. We're close, sure, but we had different mothers."

"Michael, what you're suggesting is quite out of the question," Celine said as kindly as she could. She felt sick with dismay, all appetite gone.

"I'm nothing if not persistent, Ceci," Michael warned her, lifting a hand and signalling a waiter. "We'd better order if you've got so little time. Next time I'll make it dinner. I suggest the catch of the day. Red Emperor, with whatever you fancy, vegetables, salad. Are you absolutely sure you want to run away?"

"Very sure, Michael." It was something she was good at. Running away.

CHAPTER EIGHT

CONDITIONED to heartbreak from her earliest years, Celine had developed a number of defence mechanisms which she quickly put into place. Over the following weeks she came into contact with Guy many times but managed to throw up a protective shield which he instantly detected and accepted with stunning indifference. She has hurt him once. She will never do it again. Her behaviour has always been erratic. Who should know better than he?

She ached. She was sad and angry, but it was all kept beneath a surprisingly convincing show of serenity.

Guy and Ashley! When she wasn't working like an automaton her heart and mind recoiled in horror. Theirs had *always* been a strange relationship. The love-hate Ashley spoke off. Now her worst fears had been made known to her. Ashley would do anything to get Guy. Somehow her perfect knight had succumbed. Sexual attraction could strike anyone, anywhere, anytime. Nature's driving force.

Guy. Her Guy!

To counteract her depression she undertook an intensive crash course of study on the Harcourt Langton group of companies. There were many non-property interests including a travel company, a computer company, a TV station, country newspapers and a supermarket chain. The family still held a considerable stake in a major maritime business. She thought she might do well to consider further study, perhaps in commerce law. She had no intention of sitting back and letting the men take over the empire though she fully expected to hit her head on the glass ceiling.

The weeks slid by and Christmas was upon them. She had finished her stint in accounting, not without effecting some change. Some of her ideas were being considered for incorporation into the accounting package.

The next phase of her training was the legal department where she expected to sit in as an observer. All this was to happen in the New Year. Meanwhile she rode the seesaw of emotions. At least nobody knew about it. She battled the jagged edge of distress through many a long, sleepless night. To love was to lose. Life had taught her that.

A few days before Christmas, Clive sent for her. His secretary had become strangely respectful. In no time at all Celine was shown into the chairman's office, more like a room in an exclusive gentleman's club, now Aunt Imelda had had her way with it.

Her uncle waved her down, his nose buried in the pages of a thick file. Why was he so rude? she thought. Was he trying to put her in her place? If so, he had failed. "Now then." He looked up abruptly, his expression stern. "I wanted to talk to you about what's happening at Christmas. Mother won't give me a firm answer, indeed she won't give me an answer at all." His ice-blue eyes smouldered. "I want you both at Langfield for our traditional Christmas dinner. It would be unthinkable if you didn't come. The whole family will be gathered."

Celine had one word for that. Hallelujah! "I'll speak to Grandma, Uncle Clive," she answered diplomatically, knowing her grandmother's mind.

"Good girl." Clive Langton looked mollified. "House going ahead, is it?"

Celine nodded. "Building will start in the New Year. Grandma is over the moon. Guy has designed her something special."

"Oh, he's clever!" It came out like a jealous snarl. "Too clever by half! I'll never forgive him for crueling the Manola Bay project."

"In its original form, Uncle Clive. The board voted on it."

"Ah, yes, the board!" There was a hard edge of bitterness in Clive Langton's voice. "He put in a lot of work there."

"We're talking about the most successful and prominent business people in the city. It was a wise decision. It's been applauded in the press. Harcourt Langton must be seen to respect world heritage values."

"You mean, we allowed ourselves to be scared off!" Feelings of anger and resentment continued to hold sway. "With his sympathy for the greenies, Guy will probably ruin us."

Celine shook her head but remained silent.

"One day that young man will come a cropper," Clive warned. "He's after my seat. Don't think I don't know it. *My* father made Harcourt Langton what it is, not *his*. That grandmother of his encourages him in every way she can."

"Above all, so did Grandfather," Celine pointed out quietly. "Are you enjoying life at Langfield, Uncle Clive?"

It took an extreme effort but Clive Langton calmed down. "Imelda has fixed it up unbelievably well. She's got style. We thought you might spare us a painting as an act of goodwill. You've got so many."

"Certainly, Uncle Clive. I intend to offer each member of the family a painting. As you say, there are far too many and so *valuable*. I don't want to live in a fortress."

"In safe storage aren't they?" Clive boomed, knowing perfectly well they were at a Harcourt Langton facility. "Imelda and I thought one of the Sydney Nolans. The big central Australia landscape. It would look well in my study. Imelda's had it done over."

I can imagine, Celine thought. Imelda, too, had the reputation for going over the top. "Would you have a second choice, Uncle Clive?" Celine asked politely. "I'd like to give the Nolans to the State Art Gallery."

Clive, who had been looking majestic, took an eternity to speak. "You *what*?" he cried finally, his head cocked forward in horror and alarm.

"I think it's the way to go," Celine explained in a serious voice. "Great paintings are to be enjoyed by as many people as possible, don't you think?"

"Absolute lunacy!" Clive offered. "Father would turn in his grave. He acquired the collection for the family, not for every Tom, Dick and Harry!"

"Tom, Dick and Harry *will* represent a fair proportion of the crowd, but it's not going to stop me, Uncle Clive. You had to know sometime. We have so much we can afford to share. I won't give them *all* away. I'll keep a few and the rest of the family can take a painting each. The most significant, however, will go to the gallery. We could call it the Langton Bequest."

If Celine thought that would soften her uncle his expression became even more ferocious. "Celine," he said determinedly, "I really believe if you go through with this you ought to be committed."

"You won't hear the art gallery agreeing with that. I'm sorry if you're upset, Uncle Clive, but the collection is mine. It's just too important to hang in a *house*. Ever since I can remember, Grandfather had security people crawling all over the place. I used to think one would leap out and shoot me."

"If Father had known what you intended to do he would have said 'go ahead'!"

Celine stood up. "I'll speak to Grandma about Christmas dinner, Uncle Clive. Don't be disappointed if she decides not to come."

"I didn't excuse you, young lady!" Clive Langton lashed out.

Celine whirled. "I have a *name*, Uncle Clive. I wish you'd use it." Her gentle, elegant voice darkened with resentment.

"It's your youth and stupidity that numbs me. You sit so demurely, butter won't melt in your mouth, then you tell me you're going to give away the collection. Lunacy is the word, young lady. Lunacy! It suddenly occurs to me your father was a fool, as well."

"You mean a fool as in honest, brave, independent! Isn't your greed a bit vulgar?"

"Oh, my!" Clive leaned back in his chair. "So the little kitten knows how to spit and snarl."

"I'd have to learn, wouldn't I, with *my* family?"

"Then you're completely outclassed, my dear. We're *real* tigers."

"Without teeth beside Grandfather."

Clive Langton glared at her. "You may go now, Celine. I can't recall any other member of my family being so rude to me. It was a sorry day Father left you so much power. Clearly it's gone to your head."

"I'm sorry, Uncle Clive," Celine said quietly, "but if you're going to talk down to me this is what's going to happen."

On the other side of the door she literally ran into Guy. The shock was electric. He reached out and steadied her.

"Is the sky falling?" she asked wryly.

The expression on his handsome face was dark and formidable. "If it did, *your* family wouldn't be in the clear." He grasped her wrist. "You might as well come with me." He advanced on the chairman's door.

"Mr. Harcourt, Mr. Harcourt!" Miss Forgan Smythe jumped up from behind her desk, looking as though she was coming apart around the edges. "Please let me ring through to Mr. Langton."

But Guy was blazing mad. He ignored her, if he even saw her. "Come on, Celine. You're a smart girl. You and I are going to talk to your uncle in private." Guy threw open the door and shut it firmly behind him.

Celine's last glimpse of her uncle's secretary was of an agonised woman wringing her hands. Fancy working for Uncle Clive, she thought faintly. No one could do that and remain in a mellow mood.

"See here, see here!" Clive Langton often spoke this way. He staggered to his feet, spluttering his outrage. "What the devil are you up to, Guy? What is Celine doing back when she was so anxious to leave?"

"Celine is a major shareholder in Harcourt Langton," Guy clipped. He spoke so forcibly Clive sat down heavily as though he had momentarily lost the power of his legs. "Thank you, Guy. I'm well aware of that."

"So you can't make a move without her. Or me."

Clive laughed grimly. "What is this? A consolidation of power. Could you *stand* another humiliation? Isn't Celine the little bolter?"

Celine was startled. "What's all this about, Guy?"

"What do you think it's about, Clive?" Anger flashed in Guy's brilliant, dark eyes.

"My dear boy, I've no idea!"

"Don't *dear boy* me!" Guy generated so much rage and contempt, Clive's ice-blue eyes flickered.

"A term of affection, Guy," he said, clearing his throat. "Something has obviously upset you."

"Sit down, Celine." Guy looked at her. "This may take a while. Would you like to get Nolan here?" He turned to Clive, who shrugged.

"Can't say I would. The fact is, Nolan's out to a meeting with Ian Brinkworth. They want to merge with us."

"Then forgive me for asking. Was Nolan the best person to send?"

Clive interpreted that as an insult. He flushed. "It's adding up, isn't it, Guy? *You* want to run Harcourt Langton."

"Not only want to run it, I am!" Guy announced without a moment's hesitation. "Harcourt Langton *needs* me, Clive, and you're going to step aside."

"Is there any possibility you might tell me, Guy, what's going on?" Celine asked.

He looked down at her. A ray of sunshine was touching her skin. It had the perfection of porcelain. "Remember a couple of board meetings ago when Clive had a sick turn?"

"Yes, I do!" Celine's grey eyes fled to her uncle, who seemed to be shrinking back in his chair. "We were talking about the Manola Bay project and how you could modify it to meet all environmental protection requirements. You spoke about an alternate site for the big development. Cape Clarence."

"God!" Clive writhed in his chair and covered his eyes.

"Exactly!" Guy agreed harshly. "Cape Clarence and the four hundred acres Sir Gerald bought more than twenty-five years ago. It took me a little while to unravel the complex set of manoeuvres you put in place, Clive, but at last I hit on the sole owners and partners in Nucleus Ltd. Clive and Nolan Langton."

A high flush had come to Clive's cheeks. "You'd do anything to discredit me."

"I've done nothing, Clive." Guy spoke in a terse voice. "You did it all to yourselves, but *why*? It's unethical, illegal, it's against the interests of the board and ultimately the shareholders. How did you think you were going to get away with it?"

"We did, didn't we?" Clive had raised a sweat, which dotted his brow and under his eyes. "With *all* our property holdings why did you have to hit on Cape Clarence? It was one of our *forgotten* assets.'

"You don't have the necessary vision, Clive," Guy told him bluntly. "But even then you knew *one* day it was going to be extremely valuable. Haven't you got enough?"

"We have *now*!" Clive did his best to rally. "You wouldn't know what it was like, Father doling out money in drips and drabs. He liked to keep us tied to him. We thought he'd go on forever. That parcel of land was a little protection."

"You're going to give it back, Clive." Guy looked at the older man directly. "Harcourt Langton is not going to buy it back, you're going to hand it over."

"The hell we are!" Clive laughed shortly. "You're talking millions of dollars."

"Would you and Nolan prefer to be thrown out?"

"See here, Guy." Clive sounded genuinely shocked. "We're major shareholders. Our father with your grandfather started this great firm."

"Can you imagine what he would have said, Uncle Clive?" Celine's breath caught in her throat. "You and Uncle Nolan tried to rob *Grandfather*?"

"That's an exaggeration, Celine."

"I don't think so." She shook her head. "I know you've suffered, Uncle Clive. I suffered myself at Grandfather's hands, but what you've done is *stupid* as well as illegal. I agree with Guy. You have to right this wrong and do it immediately before anyone else finds out. Can you imagine the disgrace! Clive and Nolan Langton thrown off the board of Harcourt Langton. In effect, major shareholders robbing themselves."

"You don't have any option, Clive," Guy summed it up. "Chalk it down as a hard lesson. We should really put this before the board but even Sir Gerald wouldn't have wished it."

"It should have taken you a long, long time," Clive told Guy bitterly.

"What, following the paper chase or becoming chairman?"

"Both. I have to discuss this with Nolan."

"I think I want to discuss it with Uncle Nolan myself," Celine said. "Don't think you can write me off as a Barbie doll. I have plans for Harcourt Langton myself."

"And why not?" Guy returned briskly. "I've always told you you had a good brain."

"You did when nobody else seemed to care. Certainly not my family. It's even possible later in life I might qualify for the position of chairman."

"So, let the good times roll!" Some of the hard tension had left Guy's face.

"How do I know you two are going to keep your mouths shut?" Clive was back to demanding.

"You don't know, Clive," said Guy, shrugging. "You're not hurting for money. You should retire. At any rate, this is the beginning and end of your little corrupt ventures."

Clive Langton fought hard to cover his desperate humiliation. "Return of the land, my resignation as chairman, that will clear it?"

"We'll give you a call, Uncle Clive."

"Thank you!" Clive was shocked into saying.

Miss Forgan Smythe wasn't at her desk. It was possible she had gone off sick. "You were pretty impressive in there," Celine told Guy as they walked down the silent corridor.

"What was impressive was he fell into the trap."

Celine wondered if she had heard right. "You mean, you didn't *know*?"

"I'd have forced their resignations if I had. I was acting on my strong suspicions and a certain amount of evidence. Not enough, I'm afraid. They covered their tracks extremely well. I took a calculated risk, that's all."

"It could have misfired, you know."

"It didn't." He shrugged again.

"So you have every chance of being voted chairman when the six months are up?"

"Probably, if *you* don't work too hard." His black eyes glinted. "I've always known there was a brain behind the angelic face. How's Michael?"

"All right," Celine answered casually.

"The word is you two have become very close."

"We are close. We're cousins."

"The word is he might become something else?"

"I promise you, Guy, the word's wrong. I feel sorry for Michael."

"*Tell* me about it."

"Don't be sarcastic. Michael's not doing the things he ought to be doing."

"Darling, I've known *that* ever since he started."

Celine's delicate, winged brows knitted. "There's terror in having to succeed for Michael. All the help in the world couldn't get him through university. But he did shine on the sports field. He plays a marvellous game of golf and tennis."

"As do I." Guy sounded bored. "Are you suggesting we could make a fortune?"

Celine ignored the irony. "You have a very secure sense of yourself, Guy. You were born with it. There's never been a lot of pressure on the home front. Your mother and grandmother adore you. Michael has always known he's a disappointment. I have to admit it. We're a dysfunctional family. Michael has such a poor relationship with Uncle Clive just as Uncle Clive had such a bad relationship with Grandfather."

"A little more of this, Celine, and I'll go to sleep."

"It could even explain why Michael gets into so many meaningless relationships."

"Not a one of us who couldn't be saved by the love of a good woman!" Guy glanced down at her radiant head. "My own view is Michael is deliriously in love with you."

"Don't say that! I couldn't handle it."

"Yes, you do have problems in that department. You're quite right, Celine. Michael is hungry for love and affection. Intimacy with the right woman."

"There's no intimacy between us. Nothing like that!" She shivered delicately.

"Despite which he has a very nasty habit of kissing you on the mouth."

"He's a toucher."

"Then tell him to keep his hands and his mouth to himself."

"I already have." Celine stopped walking and looked up at him. *Her* Guy. Her one perfect love. She had broken the relationship and there was no way to mend it.

"Don't look at me like that," he said, his chiselled face going taut.

She sighed. Softly, sadly. If you loved someone why couldn't you tell them?

"You have the most beautiful eyes. It's like getting lost in a mist," he murmured.

Lost in *love*. The silence grew as did the extraordinary flow of sensuality.

"I have a mild objection to being made a fool of," he rasped.

She flushed. "No one could make a fool out of you, Guy."

"Not the *second* time."

She dipped her head, the lustrous waves and curls glinting every shade of gold and copper and red. "My God, Guy, I know I should have done things differently. I've had to live with my mistake."

"So don't let's make one more."

"That won't happen." She had driven him into the arms of Ashley. "Anyway, I was trying to speak to you about Michael."

"Why do I hate myself for not finding him interesting?" Guy began to walk on.

"We have a TV station, don't we?"

"It's in South Australia. Why, are you hoping to get on it?"

Celine caught him up, her head just coming to his shoulder. "For all you know they may be genuinely pleased to see me. It's Michael I'm thinking of. He has an encyclopedic knowledge of sports. It's his one great area of expertise. His biggest enthusiasm."

"I *know*. He's often given me a bad migraine."

"You could help him, Guy. Michael has no real place here. No sense of self-esteem. There are too many brilliant people."

"Well, definitely me," Guy agreed facetiously.

"Why don't we give him a chance as a sportscaster? Is that what they call them? He looks fabulous on TV. He has an attractive speaking voice. That should win over the women viewers."

"Actually half the female population as soon as they realise his wealth."

"Wealth hasn't made any of us happy."

"It should *help*. You're serious?"

"It's only just occurred to me. I'm concerned about Michael, Guy."

"Oh, he'll survive," Guy retorted philosophically. "If only you'd felt this bad about *me*."

"But you're over me." So why did this current always crackle between them?

"Is there any good reason why I shouldn't be?" he asked airily. "I can take all your little blows without flinching."

"*Blows*? What do you mean?"

"Come on! You've got a real knack for it. Just when I thought we might be able to pick up a few pieces you go cold on the idea. I can't spend all my time trying to fathom your emotional shifts."

"Especially not when you're looking in Ashley's direction."

As always the mention of Ashley affected him powerfully. "This business with Ashley," he said tersely. "It drives me *wild*!"

"It happens though, doesn't it?" she offered sadly.

"*What* happens?" He appeared to grind his perfect white teeth. "Oh, who the hell cares!" He spun on his heel. "I'm busy, Celine. I *used* to love you. I still want you to have a long and happy life, but for God's sake, leave *me* alone."

"We used to be able to communicate, Guy," she called after him. "We've been through so much together. You were *everything* to me. Almost a brother."

He walked back to her, holding a hand to his temple. "Is this one of life's profound statements? You thought of me as a *brother*?"

"I thought of you as every important person in my life. Mother, father, the brother I never had. The most *precious* person in the world!"

"Don't cry," he said, reaching out for her at the same time.

"*Guy!*" She rested her head against his breast, dizzy with her love for him.

"My God, isn't life a struggle," he said. "I'm so used to looking out for you I can't stop."

"Be my friend," she whispered. "I can't lose you."

"You've lost *something*," said Guy. "Maybe the ability to make a commitment." His hand stroked her hair. "The fear of a little girl persists through time. Your family offered you very little. We've always recognised that. Is that the reason for all the defensive shields?" Grasping a handful of her hair, he lifted her head.

He knew all about her defensive shields, but he didn't seem to know the reason. Suddenly she wanted terribly to tell him. His eyes rested so meltingly on her face. Velvet black, deep, exquisitely passionate. They raced her pulse even as they moved her to tears. Guy was her hero, her soul. She would never change.

"*Tell* me!" His urgency dazzled her. "You can plead so eloquently for everyone else."

Her lips parted. She longed to give him the answers he was so impatient for, only the doors of the executive lift opened and Ashley stepped out, long legs flashing.

She stopped in full flight as she caught sight of them, just managing to mask her expression. Her blond hair, almost white from a tropical sun, swung around her lightly tanned face, her blue eyes glittered like icefloes with an Arctic sun on them. They all knew one another so well it was apparent she had caught the mood of extreme emotional tension.

The moment, so crucial to Celine's interests, was utterly spoiled.

In the quiet, Ashley's light, arrogant voice resounded. "This is carrying things a bit far. Shouldn't you two be working?"

"*You* want to try it," Guy remarked as though he disliked her.

"No, thank you, darling!" She gave him a brilliant, triangular smile. "My one aim in life is to enjoy myself. You have to admit I know all the right things to do."

Ashley's eyes were drilling into Guy with such intensity Celine found their expression quite scary. "So how was Fiji?" she asked in an effort to normalise the atmosphere.

"Glorious, Ceci!" At last Ashley turned to her, seeing behind Celine's assumed calm. "You should've come with me instead of playing at this ridiculous 9 to 5. I had a lovely time. An absolute idyll. Still it's wonderful to see both your faces." There was a peculiar blaze at the centre of the icefloes. "Dad busy? I don't see that old witch, Forgan Smythe. We had an appointment for lunch."

"He hasn't anyone with him at the moment," Celine volunteered.

"You're a sweet little thing, aren't you?" Ashley said in a strange voice.

"When did you recognise it?" Guy asked.

"*Spiritual*, that's it!" Ashley continued as if she hadn't heard him. "A *bright* soul. You mightn't be a Langton at all."

"Are you in some sort of crisis, Ashley?" Guy continued, still in that subtle, attacking tone.

Ashley turned to him and laughed. "You're *amazing*, Guy! You know so many things." She might as well have added, *about me*.

"Yes, Ashley, I do," he replied sombrely. "If you'll both excuse me, I must be on my way."

"You're dropping in Christmas morning, aren't you, Guy?" Ashley sought to detain him, her hand on his sleeve. "Anyway, I'll be seeing you before then."

Not if I can help it, the severity of Guy's expression seemed to say. Was he fighting to overcome this unholy attraction? Celine thought. Ashley's overt sexuality would test any man.

"Do you want to walk with me, Celine?" he asked.

"I'd like to speak to Ceci for a moment, Guy, if you don't mind."

For a moment Celine thought he was going to challenge her, but he lifted a hand in a salute and walked on to the lift.

"An odd triangle, aren't we?" Ashley murmured when they were alone.

"*Triangle*?" I can't bear to believe it, Celine thought.

"Both of us in love with Guy." Ashley spoke so softly Celine could hardly hear her. "Guy plagued by the violence of his feeling for me. He really wants to love you, Ceci, only I keep getting in the way."

Celine felt a burst of anger and jealousy as old as time itself. "I don't think think he *likes* you, Ashley. That could be the problem."

"What's liking compared to desire?" Ashley gave her a steamy look. "I wouldn't have had this happen for the world!"

"If it's not too much to ask, *what's* happening?"

"Do I have to spell it out? God, Ceci!" she muttered.

"I don't care if you *shout* it. All this secrecy. The hints, the intrigue, the lies. Why must we endlessly shuffle around in the dark? If you love Guy and he loves you, what can I do about it?"

Ashley's eyes froze. "You can leave us alone, instead of trying to get him back. But *no*! You're everywhere like some lingering perfume."

Celine was startled. "I think you overrate my power."

"You *underrate* it." Ashley cut her off. "You always did. I suppose that's a manifestation of your spirituality. You're so damned noble. Running off because you thought you weren't good enough for Guy! Who the hell else would have done that? When he called you a fool, Gramps had a point."

"I think you and Gramps would have to accept some of the blame," Celine said with a hint of disgust. "That was years ago anyway. I wasn't twenty. Not even a modern twenty. I was overprotected, over-isolated. Maybe that was why I kept trusting you. You put yourself into the role of big sister. You helped me fight out of the shadows, then you turned on me. It was Guy. When you told me so often how you disliked and mistrusted him, you wanted him with every fibre of your being."

"Not only that, I intend to get him!" Ashley's voice rose dramatically. "I don't have any of your precious scruples, as you'll discover. I don't want to hurt you, Ceci. You must believe that. I love you. You're a far better person than I'll ever be. But we have this terrible conflict."

"*You* have this terrible conflict, Ashley," Celine pointed out quietly. "I'd be happy to see if I could find you a good counsellor. It's not the first time you've fallen in love with the wrong man.''

Affronted, Ashley grasped hard at her silver earring. It fell to the floor with a clatter and she was obliged to pick it up. "You're talking affairs, Celine. Sex. I'm talking about a magnificent *obsession*! I can't remember the time when I didn't want Guy. He was the first excitement I ever had. He was fired into me. My demon lover. I used to fantasise about him endlessly. I still do.''

"Then that strikes me as extremely odd. Why would you fantasise about him when you've supposedly had the real thing?''

Ashley touched her blond hair, momentarily looking confused. "He's fighting it, Ceci. Surely you can see that? It's a classic example of a love-hate. Why are you so *blind*? Guy has to be in total control. That's one reason why he became engaged to you. You were such a sweet, compliant creature.''

Celine clicked her tongue. "You really make me sound attractive. Why don't you add 'goofy' for good measure?''

"You were never stupid, Ceci. In many ways you were extremely bright. Just not about Guy.''

"And you're the femme fatale?''

"That's how my mamma raised me!'' Ashley answered flippantly. "She never wanted me to be a *brain*.''

"Maybe that was her way of acknowledging you were never going to be a straight-A student.''

Ashley laughed, reaching out to touch Celine's cheek. "Touché, Ceci. Don't let's fight. Fighting with you is the hardest part of all. We were so close. You mean more to me than my own family. You're closer than Michael.''

"Poor Michael!" A few words could capture the essence of a life.

"And you want to watch your step there," Ashley advised, sounding, of all things, pious. "Michael fancies he's in love with you. Isn't that sick?"

"I see it as he's had precious little affection. If he could break away from the family, he might heal."

"Well, we are a terrible lot," Ashley admitted with a mirthless smile.

"You didn't know Max got engaged to Holly Lewis?" Celine slipped in so casually, Ashley answered on automatic.

"No, I didn't!"

"So that little business with the photographers didn't work."

Instantly Ashley's expression grew so uncharacteristically defensive it told Celine all she needed to know. "What photographs? What are we talking about?"

"The photographs of Max and me you sent to Guy."

Ashley arched her eyebrows high. "My dear Ceci, you're talking in riddles. I know nothing whatever about any photographs. I keep telling you you can expect that sort of thing now you're in the public eye, but you won't listen. Now, I have to pop in and collect Dad. You and Gran are coming to us Christmas Day?"

"I wouldn't count on it, Ashley."

Ashley threw her a stern, reproving look. "But we *are* counting on it. We've never missed having Christmas dinner before. We are family, you know."

"Sometimes I try to forget that," Celine said quietly, and turned away.

CHAPTER NINE

CELINE recalled with great vividness Christmas Day. Helena said from the moment she left she never intended to set foot on Langfield again and it appeared she meant it. These days Helena was acting more like a woman who had recovered from a long illness than a grieving widow. Even her mental and physical health was much improved. There was a brightness in her eyes, a sheen on her skin, a sense of purpose in her step. It was as though she had regained the good spirits and optimism of her youth.

"I'll be damned if I'm going over to Clive and Imelda," she told Celine when she broached the subject. "Not this year and maybe not ever. I want peace and tranquillity in my life. Not my overbearing, overpowering family. I resent what has been done to me and quite rightly. I've been turfed out of my own home. Not that I ever liked it much. I always expected Gerald's security people to come in and shoot me by mistake. I know you did, too."

"Could we ask them to call Christmas morning, Grandma?" Celine suggested. "They genuinely want to see us."

"That's the truly peculiar part. All right, darling, call them and ask them to pop in Christmas morning. That should do it. Make it fairly early. I've promised we'd stop over at Muriel's for a few minutes to say hello. I do so admire Muriel. I know you never knew this, the

Harcourts would never put it about, but Gerald had quite a yen for Muriel in the old days. She was such a dynamic young woman. The very antithesis of me. Of course she loved Lew. A one-man woman was Muriel and he gave her such a happy life!'' Helena sighed.

''But this is extraordinary!'' Celine said, really meaning it.

''Oh, yes.'' Helena patted the collar of the lovely blue-and-white printed dress Celine had chosen for her. ''It was a big secret even from me, but I knew. I wasn't prepared to discuss it, that's all. Not that there was anything *to* discuss. The want was all on Gerald's side, the need to best Lew, who was his very best *friend*. Your grandfather, rest his soul, was a very strange man. The strangest man I've ever known and that includes Clive. Of course it would never have worked with Muriel. They would have *roared* at each other, possibly taken to each other with whips. Such strong-minded people! I was the little puppet Gerald could put back in its box. I'm sorry to say my mother taught me to defer to my husband in all things. A crime really. Don't *ever* do it. Now I'm my own woman and I love it. Does that sound too awful, darling?''

''It sounds honest, Grandma. And sad.''

''I spent too much time brooding. It was my own fault. I should have made a life for myself.''

''It's not too late, Grandma!'' Celine took her grandmother's hand, feeling the tight, loving response.

Christmas morning, ten o'clock on the dot, the family descended on them en masse, laden down with so many presents Celine thought they were really in need of a forklift. Ritual kisses and greetings were shared. This was only done once a year. They all sat in the large, airy living room while Helena, the recipient of the bulk of the gifts, examined each present in turn.

"This is splendid, Imelda," she said of a weighty sterling-silver tureen designed like a cabbage. "Polishing it will give me something to do."

"I'm glad you like it, Mother," Imelda said, glancing sideways to try to ascertain the exact expression on her mother-in-law's face.

"It's not too late to come to us, Mother." Clive did something he hadn't done in years. He spoke kindly.

"You can't be serious staying here, Mother," added Imelda, very festive in green slacks and a red blouse with an enormous bow. "Why, it isn't even your own home!"

"I was never more serious in my life, Imelda," Helena told her daughter-in-law pleasantly. "I thought I had my own home when I married, but it appears I was wrong."

"I hate you to say that, Mother." Clive sounded desperately hurt. "You haven't been thrown out onto the streets. Father meant you to be properly looked after by us. It was entirely your own decision to set up house elsewhere."

"People need their independence, Clive. As much when they're elderly as at any other time. Oh, thank you so much, Warren," she exclaimed as her youngest grandchild came forward to present his gift. "You painted this yourself?" Helena looked up with a smile.

"What it's supposed to represent God only knows!" Ashley mocked. *It* was a small acrylic on canvas, sensitively framed.

"I call it 'Solitude', Gran!" Warren put his arms around his grandmother's frail shoulders.

"That's certainly the mood!" Celine had moved forward to study the small painting. "You have talent, Warren," she said warmly. "You should take your painting more seriously."

"Do you think so, Ceci?" Warren blushed.

"Celine is not qualified to give advice," his mother said repressively from the sofa where she was huddled up with her husband Nolan, thick as thieves. "Warren has quite enough on his hands trying to pass his exams."

"A lot of people can't paint!" Celine looked down at the canvas again. Why was Aunt Dorothy such a domineering woman? If her intention was to make Warren resent her, she was doing a great job.

When Michael gave Celine her gift, a heavy gold necklace that looked like it might have been worn by Nefertiti, he hugged her to him tightly. "With my love! That was a brainwave of yours thinking I could get a job as a sportscaster. I've already put out a few feelers and the feedback has been promising."

"I'm pleased for you, Michael." Gently Celine disengaged herself before some damage was done to her spine.

"Don't for the love of God say anything to Mum and Dad," he begged.

"I wouldn't dream of it!" Celine replied with considerable fellow feeling. "I've already been shot down for suggesting Warren might take his painting more seriously."

"Painting?" Michael laughed derisively, almost an echo of Ashley's. "No one could cop an *artist* in the family."

"When Grandfather was such a notable collector?"

"It was the money, wasn't it? Money was the big part."

"You're wrong!" Celine shook her head. "Grandfather loved his paintings."

"If you say so, Ceci. I couldn't care less about any of them. I'd sooner have action shots of my favourite football players. You're the only one of us who's genuinely artistic. The Harcourts are the real art patrons. Family tradition and all that. Guy, the brilliant architect. You expect that sort of thing. As to that, Guy can draw exceedingly good faces. He did some marvellous sketches of you. Whatever happened to them?"

"They probably got pulped."

"Or he made one big fire!" Michael grinned. "God, jilting Guy has to be the most reckless thing you've ever done. Here, let me put the necklace on for you. It cost me a pretty penny I don't mind telling you."

"A box of handkerchiefs would have done fine." Celine held up the silken masses of her hair so he could secure the catch.

"And make me look mean? You deserve the best, Ceci," he said hotly.

"Don't start talking like that, Michael," she warned him.

"It's the little glass of sherry. The last time I had sherry I was four years old and sick under the table. Did I tell you you look wonderful?"

Celine walked towards a tall, gilt-framed mirror. "A couple of times." She was wearing a very pretty sheer silk dress in a swirl of colours from pink through to violet but the necklace, far too opulent for day wear, made her look as though she was all dressed up for a party at Buckingham Palace.

"That's terrific!" Michael held her by the shoulders.

"It does indeed make a very strong statement. Thank you very much, Michael. I shall treasure this gift from my cousin. Do you mind if I take it off now? It's too decorative for day wear."

"No, *please*, leave it on!" Michael made a grab for her right arm. "If anyone can wear jewellery, you can. You have perfect skin and no amount of dazzle could top your glorious hair." His voice trailed away as Ashley in a bright red shift dress with a scalloped neckline sauntered up to them.

"I insist on knowing how much you paid for that, Michael," she said, staring at the necklace. "It looks like a stage piece. Quite bizarre!"

"Ceci loves it!" Michael responded angrily. "Why do you have to spoil things, Ashley?"

"Listen to the boy!" Ashley crowed. "It's my rotten nature. I really mean, the piece is quite spectacular."

"Promise me you won't take it off, Ceci," Michael begged as though her decision was very important to him.

"Of course, Michael." Not for anything, at that moment with Ashley looking on, could she have disappointed him.

"Thanks, Ceci," he sighed.

"That boy's heading for trouble," Ashley muttered as Michael responded to a signal from his father. "Why don't you tell him he's being absurd?"

"I'm trying to be a little kinder than that, Ashley," Celine said. "This little…whatever it is…will pass with no encouragement."

Ashley's narrow, finely shaped mouth turned down. "He's always been a bit wacko about you. We're kind of an obsessive family. The hell is, everyone tends to love you and hate me."

"You're unhappy, Ashley. You lash out. That might be part of it."

"Do you ever say *anything* nasty?" Ashley smiled.

"I once hissed at a young punk who tried to steal my bag."

"I wish you were coming over, Ceci." Ashley sounded genuinely regretful.

"I can't leave Grandma."

"Why the hell not? Gran is dreary at the best of times."

"No, she *isn't*! She can be very funny."

"You'd have fooled me." Ashley shrugged. "So why not come over tonight? Stay the night. We have so much to catch up on and you'll love what Mamma has done to the house."

"I'll come soon, Ashley," Celine promised. "Not tonight."

"I bet you're going to the Harcourt's New Year's Eve party, Gran or not?"

"I've been invited." Celine met her cousin's ice-blue eyes.

"We've *all* been invited," Ashley mocked. "It's obligatory, don't you know. We're Harcourt Langton, after all, though that could change if our Guy has his way. Can't you see it at the front of the building in big, tall brass letters. The Harcourt Corporation?"

"He might like it, but I think we'll manage to keep the Langton alive."

Ashley's mood switches were amazing. "Sweet Ceci, you astonish me!" she said on a wave of laughter. "Have you any plans to see Guy today?"

"I expect I will for a short time," Celine answered casually. "Grandma traditionally sees Muriel and Eloise Christmas morning for a quick hello."

"Do you mind if I tag along after you?" Ashley asked. "I promise I'll leave after I give Guy his present."

"But you never give presents to the Harcourts, Ashley?"

Ashley thought a minute before she answered. "If one *starts* giving presents, where does it all end? I've never thought Muriel and Eloise liked me. I could be wrong. As for Guy! This year it's different. I really want to give him something he'll treasure."

"Are we talking an object of great rarity?" Celine asked more tartly than she intended.

"Wait and see." Ashley smiled.

It simply wasn't possible to make any further objection.

Eloise, a beautiful, retiring woman whose life had been blighted by the early tragic death of her husband, greeted them with open pleasure and no hint of surprise Ashley had tagged along.

Kisses were exchanged Euro-style; seasonal greetings.

"Muriel is waiting for us in the drawing room," Eloise told them with her gentle smile. As usual she was beautifully dressed, her taste as quietly elegant as Muriel's was dramatic. "Guy hasn't arrived yet. He's taken Greg Maitland to the airport. Greg's having Christmas dinner in Sydney with his parents."

In the gracious Harcourt drawing room with its soaring ceiling and grand dimensions Muriel sat enthroned like a queen before the splendid fireplace. The mantelpiece behind her was adorned with a fabulous decorative Christmas swag featuring dark evergreen foliage, gold and scarlet baubles, Christmas angels, bows and tassels and tiny, sumptuously wrapped presents tied with scarlet ribbons. It was a work of art and Celine exclaimed aloud.

"Guy's idea this year." Muriel beamed. "Doesn't it give such a festive look to the room?"

"Guy's *idea*, Eloise put in a lot of time getting it all together." Muriel rose to greet them, giving Eloise a warm, loving look. "Our house is always beautiful with Eloise in it. She arranged all the flowers, as well." She gestured around the room at the strikingly beautiful arrangements, all continuing the festive air.

Helena almost moaned. If only she'd had a daughter-in-law like Eloise! Muriel genuinely loved her like a daughter. The two women had lived together in perfect harmony since the Harcourts' double tragedy. It was true Muriel had wanted her daughter-in-law to remarry and pick up the shattered pieces of her life, but something vital in Eloise had died with her husband.

Helena looked at her lifelong friend Muriel with a little smile. Even in her mid-seventies Muriel's looks were dramatic. Today she wore a wondrous Middle Eastern type garment, obviously of her own design, with a necklace of gold links at her throat. Her presence had a *force* that was palpable. Muriel had passed it on to her grandson along with her glossy, crow-black hair and the brilliant midnight dark of the eyes.

"I bet you weren't expecting to see me, Lady Harcourt." Ashley gave her curious little crack of laughter.

"You're very welcome, Ashley, at any time," Muriel said graciously. As fibs went it was a great success, for the sophisticated Ashley blushed with pleasure.

Muriel saw them all comfortably seated, then almost on cue, Maybelline, the Harcourt housekeeper, wheeled in a trolley laden with the silver tea service, exquisite Spode china and a selection of mouth-watering little pastries and small cakes.

"A choice of teas." Muriel smiled, preparing to do the honours. "Your favourite, Lapsang Souchong, Helena, dear, and a particularly fine quality Darjeeling."

Ashley looked like she wanted to laugh. Tea wasn't her favourite beverage.

Afterwards presents were exchanged. A Hermès scarf somehow materialised for Ashley, who eyed it so intently it might well have been a bomb. Celine was rather embarrassed by Ashley's manner. Ashley wouldn't have come at all, only for *Guy!*

Celine's gift to Eloise was a small bronze head of a boy. It had reminded her of Guy the moment she laid eyes on it amid an array of small artworks in an antique shop. Eloise saw the resemblance, too, because she held it to her heart.

"This is truly beautiful, Celine," she said, her large, grey-green eyes misted over. "It might almost be Guy at the same age."

"That's what drew me to it." Celine didn't realise how revealing was her expression until Ashley gave another one of her ironic laughs.

"It's been difficult for you to get over Guy, hasn't it, Ceci?"

"Guy and Celine will always care about each other, Ashley," Eloise said quietly.

Celine's gifts included a Bally handbag and a beautiful gold lace vest which she thought she could team with her wide-legged evening trousers.

Guy arrived ten minutes later, like his mother and grandmother, betraying no hint of surprise at Ashley's unexpected appearance.

"Happy Christmas, darling!" she said boldly, handing him a richly gift-wrapped box.

"This is such a surprise, Ashley!" He took the box into his fine hands. "The first Christmas present I've ever had from you."

"And not the last! I've gone to considerable trouble choosing it." She gave him a brilliant smile.

There was a kind of wariness in Guy's expression. While they all watched he unwrapped the box, put the paper and trimmings down on a small table then lifted out a silver-gilt goblet Celine thought for one minute might have gone missing from a cathedral.

"This is really something, Ashley!" Guy looked down at her. "I'm only *asking*, mind you, is it a liturgical vessel?"

"Of course it's not!" Ashley said a touch anxiously. "What made you think of *that*?"

He shrugged. "It sprang to mind at first sight. I think those grapes and wheat ears mean something."

"I knew you'd love it." Ashley placed a beautifully manicured hand on his arm. "It's supposed to date from the eighteenth century."

"When my wits settle, I'll thank you," he said crisply. "I can't produce a similarly unique gift for you but you must allow me to find you something you can admire."

"I'd rather see *you* happy." She flashed him another of her brilliant smiles. "Now I really must go. Mamma will expect me home to lend a hand. I saw you looking at Celine's necklace, Guy, when you came in. It's fabulous, isn't it? Maybe a touch heavy. Ceci and

Michael have certainly come a long way. I've never seen Michael so over the moon!"

"I'll walk you to the door, Ashley," Guy said.

"Lovely!" She looked up at him with lazy sensuality. "Have a wonderful day, everybody. It might be a touch gloomy for Gran and Ceci, but not even Michael could persuade them to come to us."

"What's all this talk of Michael?" Muriel asked in some astonishment as Guy escorted Ashley to her car.

Helena answered, putting it in polite terms. "Ashley can be very naughty when she wants to be. Michael has been a little in love with Celine since they were children. A puppy love sort of thing. My own theory is Celine was always so sweet to him when his sister was a little monster. Now Ashley's putting it about they're having a romance. It's all for effect."

If that's what it was, it was getting results, Celine thought. Guy's dark eyes had been locked on Michael's gift as soon as he'd entered the drawing room. He even looked as though he knew who had given it to her. *Why* had she promised Michael she would wear it all day? It was too heavy, too *gleaming*. It just could spoil things.

"I do wish you could stay and have Christmas dinner with us," Muriel was saying. "Ashley's right, in a way. It will be quiet for you."

Helena shook her head regretfully. "Thank you so much, Muriel, but I think I've given the family enough of a shock. They would be mortally offended if I declined their invitation and stayed here."

"Of course, my dear. Well, come along and see the dining room, anyway. Eloise has worked magic."

While the others moved into the dining room to admire the festive decorations and the table, Celine edged towards the French doors that led out onto the loggia and the blazing summer gardens beyond. She was a little ashamed of her action, but she was desperate to see how Guy and Ashley acted towards each other when they thought themselves alone. There was such a sense of confusion, even disbelief, mixed up with her feelings of loss and betrayal. Ashley could weave such a web of deceit. The most terrifying thing was she was often believed. How well she remembered the distraught weeks before she had broken off her engagement. Behind Ashley's counselling had been a sinister self-interest. Behind the smiling face, the dark shadows.

The rich, beguiling scent of the roses wafted to her nostrils. There were at least a hundred varieties in glorious display; hybrid tea roses, floribundas, old-fashioned roses, climbers trained over arches, the great double hedges of the pure white Iceberg leading down to the octagonal summer pavilion where Guy first told her he loved her.

He had meant it. *Then*. His eyes had held such intensity and passion she had lost herself in their dark spell.

Now Ashley and Guy were standing close together beside Ashley's brand new B.M.W. Even to someone not familiar with them, there was acute tension in their body language. It was like looking at lovers in the midst of a furious quarrel. Ashley was staring up into Guy's face, her blond hair lifting in the breeze and fanning across one cheek. She jerked it away and Celine caught her expression. It was *raw* with feeling. She wouldn't have believed it had she not seen it with her own eyes. Ashley who had given voice to a thousand denials was madly, terribly, in love with Guy. For a moment the compassionate Celine felt a great burst of pity. Ashley was in agony. Wanting to be loved, she must be finding Guy was having difficulty with the relationship.

Almost in a state of hypnosis, Celine watched as Guy turned away, his handsome face dark and stormy. Ashley stumbled after him, catching at his arm. Celine thought Ashley was crying. Ashley, her cousin. Ashley who had filled the role of big sister. The fact she was a traitor didn't strip away the old affection from Celine's tender heart. Ashley was far more vulnerable than Celine would ever have believed.

Was it possible Guy sought to humiliate her? He wasn't normally callous, but, drawn to her against his will, did he deeply resent her compulsive hold on him? Was the rage all against himself? There was *something* peculiar about the intensity of his feeling. In her passion Ashley had flung up an arm, catching at Guy's head. He threw it off, yet with the strength of desperation Ashley succeeded in pulling his head down to her, rising on tiptoe to seize the exquisite warmth of his mouth.

Not even Guy was proof against such temptation, Celine thought. She turned away abruptly, trembling with shock. Ashley went after what she wanted just as their grandfather had. Both of them predatory people with remarkable needs.

Celine's joy in the beautiful day turned to ashes. For each of us comes the moment, she thought. The moment when we know we've lost our one chance at true happiness.

From close by she heard her grandmother asking to see the roses. Moments later she caught sight of the three ladies strolling contentedly down the famous Iceberg Walk. The flowering was prolific. Masses and masses of pure white roses, a spectacle beautiful enough to stop the heart with delight. It didn't seem unusual they had wandered off. Obviously it was intended she have a private moment with Guy.

From somewhere on the terrace she heard him call her name, then he appeared at the French doors. He still had a brooding expression on his marvellous face.

"Everything okay?" she forced herself to ask.

His sudden smile was like the sun breaking through clouds. "The girls are working in together. They've gone off to see the roses so we can be alone."

"That seems to be the idea. Enjoy seeing Ashley off?"

"My God! What a character she is. A real case!"

"You look tense."

"I assure you I wasn't before Ashley showed up with that chalice. Do you suppose she stole it?"

Celine shrugged. "It might be worth knowing where she got it from."

"And your necklace!" Guy said suavely. "Tell me about it. It looks like it might have been lifted from an Egyptian tomb."

"Michael and Ashley seem to have similar taste." Celine glanced down at the wide, glittering band.

"Indeed they have." Guy moved towards her. "They bring to mind Sir Gerald at his most flamboyant. Helena told me the other day she's going to have her diamond solitaire cut off."

"Well, I know who'll be there to catch it. Ashley adores it."

He smiled wryly. "I can't think why. Helena always disliked it but Sir Gerald insisted she wear it. Don't you think now we've all admired your necklace you could take it off?"

"Michael asked me, begged me really, to keep it on," she said a little shakily.

"I'm not sure I'm ready to listen to that. Since when have you obeyed Michael's every fond wish?"

That deep humming current of sexual energy was pulsing between them. "It seemed important to him." Celine advanced, conscious she was provoking him but unable to stop it.

"Let's try to get it off, shall we? It looks too heavy for your slender neck."

His determination was apparent so she lifted the masses of her hair and presented him with her pearly neck.

"Do I leave your gold chain or not?"

"Leave it," she said, easing out a ragged breath.

"It's unclear why you still wear it." He released the catch of the heavy gold necklace, unburdening her of its almost oppressive weight.

"In memory of the old magic," she heard herself saying. She let her hair fall once more around her shoulders, lifting her head and seeing them both reflected in a tall, giltwood mirror that stood atop a handsome console. They looked rather magical in the antique, silvery glass. Perfect foils. At the height of summer Guy's olive skin had a rich, golden sheen, hair, brows, brilliant eyes, a gleaming black. She looked almost ethereal in contrast, a gossamer creature with a long, graceful neck and slender arms. She had lived protected from the sun so her skin remained porcelain, her long, red-gold mane a blazing radiance.

That used to be us, she thought. Guy and Celine. Soon to be married. She made a little involuntary heartbroken sound, then, realising it, ducked her head.

"Regrets, Celine?" he asked, with his uncanny ability to read her mind.

"A few."

"All the days, the nights, the weeks, months and years you've been away from me," he said in a low, intense voice.

Tears formed in her cloud-soft grey eyes. One trailed down her cheek.

"You used to fit into my arms as though you *belonged*."

"I suppose I do still," she whispered.

"Except there's no happy ever after!" He moved behind her, encircling her willowy body with characteristic mastery. "I should have held you fast," he muttered. "I should have taken you, made you pregnant if I had to, instead of all this torment!"

Her senses were flooded with bittersweet nostalgia. Her head fell back irresistibly. Came to rest against his shoulder. Her tender mouth opened like a flower.

"What is it you're offering?" he asked harshly. His hand moved, caressed her delicate breast.

The sensual arousal was so powerful she gasped. "I can't bear the thought I've hurt you."

"You'd do it again," he said tautly, yet covered her mouth with a kiss that betrayed a deep, silent hunger.

How could they solve this? It seemed impossible.

The New Year came in promising big things for Harcourt Langton. Approval had been granted by the Fiji government for an international tourist and residential development on one of their beautiful islands. Celine had already studied the project in detail; the executive summary, the financial report, and Guy's brilliant design plans. It was a major development on a spectacularly beautiful site.

Clive Langton had already announced to a stunned board he wouldn't be standing for the position of chairman at the end of his six-month stint which was drawing to a close. He had put it about he wanted to ease the workload, leaving some to speculate he might fear a heart attack. It was well known he suffered from high blood pressure. This left the way clear for Guy. The Cape Clarence parcel of land, once more a company asset, would be developed at some future time.

On a more modest level, Helena's new house was rapidly taking shape. While Celine was at work, Helena and her ever-faithful Goldie had taken to driving over every day to check on work in progress. Both women enjoyed themselves immensely with their innocent, new-found pleasures.

"I can't wait until the roof goes on," Helena told Celine cheerfully. "We'll have a little party."

Celine had deliberately missed the New Year party at Harcourt House. She felt miserable about it, she hated telling lies, but she'd invented a migraine. She had suffered migraines on and off throughout her life, so as an excuse it was plausible enough, except her decision did its own damage.

Guy became more mettlesome than ever. His natural wit found a devastating sharpness that sometimes took Celine right to the edge. In the following months his photograph appeared many times in the newspapers, in the business section and in the social pages. On two occasions he was photographed with the same brunette, a partner in a public relations firm; another two had him with an incredibly glamorous-looking Ashley at his side.

Celine well remembered the particular functions. She had been invited to both and attended for a very short time, dodging Guy, her family, and the photographers all the while.

True to her promise Helena gave a little party for the workmen when the house was finished. She stayed to sip a glass of champagne and afterwards Celine drove her home. Guy had been invited as a matter of course but at the last moment he had been called away to confer with their senior engineer on an onsite problem. Traffic had held Celine up so she didn't get to see as much as she wanted to, so Helena gave her a set of keys to look over the house at her leisure the following afternoon.

Her first thought was Guy had created a grand feeling in a compact space. Helena had wanted a "small" house, or what she considered small, which was a lot of house to most people. Guy had come up with a masterpiece of modern design, yet classical in its symmetry and without the corridors Helena had hated at Langfield. The master bedroom, library, living and dining rooms were aligned along the length of the lot to take advantage of the view of the river and the parkland on the opposite bank filled with towering blue gums and acacias that in winter turned the natural reserve into a soft golden glory.

Celine wandered around the silent rooms, feeling Guy's presence beside her. How well she knew and loved his great gift. Late afternoon sunlight slanted in through the floor-to-ceiling glass doors that led from the main rooms onto the spacious rear terrace. She unlocked one door and walked out, moving dreamily across the thick, springy grass. Six-foot-high fences in white-rendered brick and wrought iron divided the house from its neighbours on both sides. This was a long established area.

Her grandmother's house was actually built on what was once the tennis court and part of the garden of the house to the left. The wrought iron on both sides was ablaze with thick bracts of the showy pink bougainvillea. At the bottom of the garden banks of blue and white hydrangea continued to bloom, sheltered to one side by a massive jacaranda that at Christmas had borne pink flowers instead of the familiar lavender-blue. Her grandmother had already engaged a well-known designer renowned for her "romantic" gardens to draw up a plan. There was to be a "white" garden, a scented garden, and a sitting arrangement down by the river, as silver as a smoked mirror with the rays of the sun on it. It was a beautiful, peaceful spot, the house a delight after the fortresslike grandeur and opulence of Langfield.

She had just reached the open doorway leading in to what was to be the master bedroom when she was arrested by the sound of footsteps coming through the house. She stood poised like a fawn, nerve endings tense, until a man came into view and she looked straight into Guy's brilliant eyes.

"Hello," she said brightly, except her heart was hammering and her blood was shooting sparks.

He didn't answer for a moment, just staring at her, half in and half out of the sunlight. "Where have you been hiding all this time?" He started towards her, his blazing vitality never more apparent.

She caught her lower lip between her teeth. She felt trapped, yet savouring a fierce happiness, the physical exhilaration of being alone with him. "I've been busy, Guy," she evaded, when she was filled with torrents of words and emotions and no way to express them. "I thought you wanted me to take my job seriously?"

His beautiful mouth twitched. "Not to the extent you show the rest of us up. I thought I'd take the opportunity to look over the house. I'm sorry I missed Helena's little party."

"She understands. Did you manage to solve the problem?"

A frown appeared between his brows, a look of determination. "We're working on it. There are a lot of hazards in construction."

"Yes." Celine looked away. No one would know better than Guy, who had lost his father. "The house is marvellous," she told him, trying to will the tumult inside of her to die down. "I love it. So does Grandma."

"It must seem like a playhouse after Langfield." He gave a lazy smile.

"That's exactly what Grandma wants. Even entering the front door one feels joyful."

"No higher praise!" Guy glanced out at the rear terrace which he had designed as an outdoor living room with tall pillars supporting the sky-lit roof. "What it really needs out here is a reflecting pool running the length of the living, dining rooms. Helena would enjoy it. I've overscaled the windows and doorways, as you can see. It adds to the feeling of spaciousness. Helena wouldn't have found it as easy as she thinks coming down to normal scale."

"She's wonderfully happy about everything, Guy. She can't wait to move in."

"So, how long are you two going to stay together?" he asked, turning a searing gaze on her. "Until some man with an exceptionally high degree of commitment sweeps you off your feet."

"*You* did." Once said there was no way to call the words back.

"And look where it got me." Immediately Guy's expression was back to taunting awareness. "Do you still wear my ring? May I see it?"

"I'm *not* wearing it, you might as well know!" She stepped back very quickly so the full blaze of the setting sun engulfed her. It radiated light from her body and turned her hair into a fiery cloud.

"God, Celine," he murmured feelingly, "seeing you now is like witnessing the sudden visit of an angel. Is it any wonder you send shivers down my spine?"

He sounded as though he really meant it but then she knew her physical beauty had always moved him. She, his bright angel. Ashley, his torment.

"It's my colouring," she managed to say.

He shrugged as though the brief moment had passed. "Well, Titian hair *is* a mark of extraordinary beauty." He reached out idly and brushed away a cobweb that had already formed on the exterior wall. "I ran into Michael before I left. He's all excited about the weekend."

"Why, what's on?" Now he wasn't about to touch her, the hammering of her heart slowed.

"Aren't you two going out on his boat? Cruising the islands?"

"Of course I'm not!" She made the mental note to tell Michael to stop making things up.

"You really should tell Michael," Guy said, sounding cynical.

"Or maybe Michael should tell me."

"Surely you're not saying he was *lying*?"

Celine hesitated. "What Michael *wants* to happen, he convinces himself is true."

"That's definitely *Ashley*," Guy said with some fervour. "Let's face it, some of your family are quite odd."

Her grey eyes darkened. "We *all* do strange things, Guy. Even *you*!"

"Mention one," he challenged her bluntly. "*What* strange thing, Celine?"

She thought only of *one*. "You have a very curious relationship with Ashley."

Even the sound of her name made his lean body tense. "Would that have anything to do with *you*?" he asked coldly.

"I have to leave now, Guy." She felt ragged with emotion, close to tears. "I'm taking Grandma and Goldie to the ballet tonight. It's the first time Grandma has been out."

"I won't keep you." She heard the terseness in his voice.

"Goodbye, then." She took a deep breath and went to move past him, her creamy skin pale.

He grasped her arm, staring down into her face. "Do you *still* wear my ring?" His question rang with challenge.

She felt her emotional control slip from her. "What do you think I am, a masochist?"

He raised his black brows. "I suppose you could be. I hadn't figured it from that angle. Weren't *you* the one to inflict pain?"

"For which you will never forgive me until hell freezes over."

"So there it is!" he agreed. "I have to admit it went deep as you might discover if you ever allow yourself to love."

"I *loved* you!" She lifted her shimmering eyes.

"Extraordinary!" It came out as total disbelief. He lifted his hand to her throat. She was wearing a sunflower-yellow silk shirtdress with several strings of necklaces around her neck. He wound his fingers through the multicoloured swirls until he isolated the gold chain that held his ring.

"Don't do this to me, Guy!" Beset by emotion, Celine tried to break away, only he compelled her back against the wall.

"Why do *you* do *this*?" he countered in an intense voice. He let the exquisite ring come to rest in the palm of his hand. "You must wear it every day of your life. I see the gold chain all the time. *My* ring nestling between your breasts. It doesn't make sense."

"It makes sense to me. You gave it to me. It belongs to me. Do you want it back?"

He grasped a handful of her hair, making her look up at him. "If I said I wanted *you* back, what would you say?"

Her mouth trembled. "I'd say it couldn't work." There was sadness in her voice, deep and constant.

"Tell me *why*?" he demanded in fierce frustration. "Stop struggling, Celine. I don't want to hurt you. I want to understand. What *is* it you can't tell me?"

She tried to turn her head away. "It's complex. You know that."

"I know you're still the lost child who can't find her way. Too much love means too much pain. You *did* love me, didn't you? I couldn't have mistaken it. It shone out of your eyes. How can so much love be lost? How could it have ended like that? *Tell* me. I can't bear not to know." His voice resonated with the emotions that burned in him.

She looked up at him directly. "I loved you, Guy, far more than you will ever know."

"And just to prove it, you fled me, without words, without an explanation. Just some strange gibberish, half hysteria, I was supposed to accept?"

Frantically she shook her head. "So many factors went into my decision, Guy. The way I was brought up. I was too young, too vulnerable, too full of private doubts."

"Then why the hell haven't you overcome them?" Goaded beyond endurance, he gave in to the overwhelming impulse to shake her.

She seemed to slump against him and he stopped. "Oh, Guy, *don't*! You accuse me of fleeing you, but what was your truth? What is it now?"

His answer was stark and immediate. He lifted her head, his fingers hard along her jawbone, crushing her mouth beneath his just as he crushed her resistance.

"I'll never be free of you, *never*!" he muttered, his mouth covering every inch of her face and throat. "Sick of you. Sick with you. Sick of the long, lonely nights. The whole wretched business." His hands smoothed her body urgently, her breasts, inciting her flesh. He had touched her like that once before. Her recollection was vivid, timeless in its power. It had stayed with her every day, the angry ecstasy, her sensation of utter defencelessness.

"You were too innocent to take *then*." Guy gave voice to a restraint that had tested him. "But you're a woman now."

Celine felt the great wave of desire coming for her, deep yet towering. She let him slip the buttons of her dress, cup her breast in a bra so thin it might have been a second skin.

"*Guy!*" She was seduced into a long, trembling sigh.

He stared down into her upflung face, her full, sensitive mouth faintly swollen from the violence of his kisses. "I don't know what's worse," he raged, "being with you, or being without you!" Yet the touch of his hand, the manipulation of her tightly furled nipple, was delicately, *exquisitely*, strong and arousing. She felt the pull of it at her body's core.

He continued to excite her until she had a sensation of falling and locked her hands behind his neck. Their bodies were crushed together as though he sought to make them one. The flame of love in her heart rose high. She had been betrayed and inarticulate those years ago, she had to speak now.

Celine threw back her head, thinking the expression in her eyes mirrored the love in her soul. "*Please*, Guy!" She was pleading to overcome her doubts and anxieties, only he took it as a familiar manifestation of withdrawal.

"Don't *stop* me," he gritted, his handsome face full of a terrible frustration. "I just might strangle you. You deserve it."

"No—*no!*" She covered his mouth with the pearly tips of her fingers. "I want to tell you how I feel. How I felt *then*."

"A miracle!" He laughed bitterly, extraordinarily on fire.

"Please listen, Guy. I couldn't properly express my love, my terrible self-doubts."

"You're telling *me*?" The midnight eyes were brilliant with remembered pain and humiliation. "There ought to be a law against women being able to do so much damage."

"I'm so sorry," she murmured, broken-heartedly. "How long do I have to pay for it?"

Abruptly his hands caught her face, cupping it, a certain pressure in his grip. "Never leave me," he said.

She was stunned by his words, the burning look in his eyes. "Guy?"

"You heard me," he said tautly. "I can't really say I love you, although I've loved you for most of your life. I know the bitter taste of rejection. It's still in my mouth. But things are a little different now. I've divined your secret. I'm prepared to live with it."

"*Secret*?" Her eyes glistened as though he had stabbed her to the heart.

"Celine, don't let's pretend anymore," he groaned. "You're terrified of being loved. You're terrified of returning it. It's a reaction to your childhood tragedy. You've carried the terror since you were six years old. You came closest to loving me but I wanted you totally. Body and soul. You couldn't handle any of it. You ran away."

"It wasn't as simple as that," Celine said in a low voice. "I admit to bouts of panic, a fear of being dominated in our relationship..."

"Is there any other man you've been drawn to?" Ruthlessly he cut her off.

"No." She shook her head. She hadn't even toyed with the idea.

"So you're still a virgin?"

"And if I *am*? Surely that's not a scandal?"

"It could mean you can't conceive of loving."

"I love you," she said very quietly.

His lean body went very still. "You just could go to hell for lying."

"I'm *not*!"

"Prove it. Marry me. It's up to you. But, lady, never run away from me again."

She shivered, knowing she was approaching a subject fraught with danger, but one that had to be addressed. "And what about Ashley?"

Convulsively he threw her off. "I *detest* Ashley," he said, white teeth gritted. "I never liked her when we were children. Now I positively loathe her."

That could well be true. "Is it possible that you also *desire* her?" Celine asked, just a little afraid of him, as though she had brought out the *wildness* beneath the so-civilised veneer.

For answer he paced halfway across the room, putting her in mind of a highly strung racehorse full of power and recklessness. "Steady," he was saying to himself. "Steady." He swung on her, his polished skin sheened with the heat of their love-making. "I desire Ashley like the proverbial hole in the head," he said in his most cutting voice. "You're *amazing*, Celine, you really are. A few minutes ago I was mad to have *you*. Mad. Enraged, obsessed. Nobody else can do it to me. And you're talking *Ashley*?"

Wretchedly she persisted. "We must face this, Guy. She loves you."

He came right up to her, his height and splendid physical fitness never more accentuated. "Celine, listen *hard*. Ashley believes, like your grandfather did, they've only got to want a thing badly enough and it's theirs.

Determination is the thing. I saw it time and time again. Determination and some kind of malignant desire to take something of value from someone close to them. It may seem unlikely to you now, but *your* grandfather got up to every strategy possible to try to break up my grandparents' engagement. It may shock you, but it's true. Delve any deeper and we'll open up a Pandora's box. I know your loyalties go deep, at least to *Ashley*, certainly not *me*, but how can any man deal with a woman like that? She spends her time fantasising, romanticising, inventing all kinds of crazy scenarios. She really ought to write books. Hell!'' He looked away, his expression plagued. ''Listen to me trying to explain something to someone who can't or won't listen. Ashley is your blood, but she's not your friend. I've warned you before.''

''And I really did listen, Guy,'' she protested.

''Rubbish!'' he said deliberately. ''You're far more prepared to believe Ashley than you'd ever believe me. I suppose that's the way of it with liars. They score far too many victories. It happens every day.''

''I'm sure of it!'' Celine agreed. ''But, Guy, I saw you both Christmas morning, when you walked Ashley to her car.''

''Ah, the new B.M.W. That should make her more dangerous. Ashley is the last woman to put in a high-powered car.''

''You can't have been arguing fiercely about *that*?''

''No, her new car didn't make me blazing mad,'' he returned shortly.

''She kissed you.''

''Shock, horror! How could you have known? Were you *spying* on us, Celine?''

She flushed at his look of open contempt, the colour staining her porcelain skin. "My only excuse is, since I've been home, a number of people have told me you and Ashley are having a relationship."

"Who are these people, Celine? If you tell me Ashley, it's likely I'll need a straitjacket."

"Ashley was only one of them."

His striking face registered disdain. "Why did I have the feeling she was? So that condemns me, does it? Honestly, Ashley's a real snake. If she were a man she'd get one where it hurts and that would be the end of it, but a man's got lots of problems with women. Especially ones who live to stir up trouble. I suppose in your simple-mindedness you didn't consider it might be to their advantage to make me the prime suspect?"

Celine shook her aching head. "Guy, the whole issue has kept me awake at nights."

"That's okay. I don't sleep that well, either."

"It wasn't *impossible*?"

"Sure. I kept telling Ashley to get lost, but she was certain that meant I loved her. Actually she's not the only one in your family who's crazy."

"Isn't that the truth!" Celine agreed miserably. "So you *deny* any relationship with her?"

His eyes flashed a deeply felt resentment. "You stand there accusing me like a solemn *child*. Who needs it? You're a woman now. When are you going to put faith in your own judgment? I'm not going to spend my time trying to clear my name. Of what, for God's sake? Your cousin Ashley has always been eaten up with jealousy. I remember, if you don't, how she always tried to diminish your pleasure in anything. Some little snide comment followed by her familiar laugh. I refuse point-blank to tolerate your mistrust when one of *your* relatives needs intensive psychiatric help. You've only seen me gentle with you up until now. Maybe that's hindered your development. But get *this*. I want you now and I'm going to have you. Think of it as shock therapy. Now run away and tell Ashley. That should bring on some loopy reaction.''

CHAPTER TEN

IT WAS mid-afternoon Saturday when Ashley decided to visit them, hard on the heels of Michael, who found it difficult to accept Celine didn't want to go out with him on the boat.

"No romancing you, Ceci," he promised her. "I'll keep my hands to myself, right?"

"Why did you tell Guy I was going out with you this weekend?" she challenged him directly.

Michael shrugged. "So I could get back at him a little. Guy's got everything. Looks, brains, charisma. Just tell me he hasn't got *you*?"

Celine shook her head. "I can't do that, Michael."

"But you rejected him?" Michael frowned, concentrating intently on her. She was wearing a long, jersey, slip dress the colour of Parma violets that turned her grey eyes iridescent.

"*Never*, Michael. I allowed myself to be *frightened* off."

"Does this involve my sister in some way?" Michael looked a little shaken.

"You know Ashley better than I do."

"Well, she's always been your rival," Michael said dully. "I can't change your mind to come with me?"

Celine strolled with him to the veranda, gently touching his arm. "I'm always your friend, Michael, but you must get on with your life. One day soon you'll find the right woman, then you'll be amazed you thought of me.''

"I don't think so, Ceci." Michael put his arm around her willowy body and gave her an expansive hug. "There's never going to be anyone like you. By the way, I've taken a step nearer to my television career. I've been asked to do a mock-up."

"When's this?" Celine looked up, warm lights in her eyes.

"End of next week. Friday. You're the only one who knows."

"Congratulations!" She gazed at him with open pleasure. "I think this could be the start of a whole new life."

"And if it is, I have you to thank." Michael couldn't bear not to kiss her cheek, savouring the scent of her skin. "I'm not looking forward to telling Dad."

"It's your life, Michael. Time to get involved in something you care about. Time to go after that worthwhile woman. They're out there. Just remember they have certain expectations."

"I can make a commitment, you know," Michael said. "I just want someone to *need* me. Not the money and so forth."

"Then nurture the right woman. You'll find someone special."

"What a tragedy you're my cousin," he said dryly, walking down the steps to his car.

"Yes, Michael," Celine called softly. "We're very, very close."

She waved him off, hoping her words and her attitude had finally sunk in. With the promise of a new job where he could actually perform well, Michael might see life altogether differently. Not that he wouldn't have a battle royal with his father. Celine could see where she would get the blame. It was unlikely she would ever have a good relationship with most of her family but that's the way it was.

Thirty minutes later Ashley arrived, a spectacle witnessed by Goldie. Celine and her grandmother were in the comfortable family room going through swatches of fabrics to pick out what they most liked for sofas, curtains and bedspreads for the new house. It was a pleasant and absorbing task and when Goldie tapped on the door, both women gave a little start.

"Yes, Goldie?" Helena looked up.

"Ashley's arrived in her plush new car. I clocked her at one hundred miles per hour through the front gate. It's a mercy it was open."

"She does drive too fast," Helena said worriedly. "Tell her to come through, would you, Goldie?"

Sprightly Goldie nodded laconically. "I think she's found something important to talk about, maybe."

Ashley made quick work of visiting her grandmother.

"Have a good time last night, Gran?" she asked, giving Helena a quick peck on the cheek. "Ballet's not my scene."

"Too many parties are not a good idea," Helena retorted. "Michael told us it broke up around 3:00 a.m.?"

"So?" Ashley shrugged. "Life's too short not to make the most of it. Are you coming over for an hour, Celine?" she demanded. "You promised."

"You mean, Langfield?" Celine felt an involuntary clutch of dismay.

"Where else? Everyone is agreed Mamma has made a marvellous job of the place," she added blithely, ignoring her grandmother's feelings on the matter.

"As long as you can live with it, Ashley," Helena responded tartly.

"No offence, Gran." Ashley gave her mocking smile. Like Celine, she was dressed for the heat in a sleeveless blue dress as light as a zephyr. "Sure you won't come with us?"

"I didn't really know I'd received an invitation?"

"Do family need that?"

"Not a one of us should forget our manners."

"What happened about Michael?" Ashley glanced away from her grandmother to ask. "I thought he was supposed to be taking you out on the boat?"

"That doesn't ring too true, Ashley." Helena sat back in her chair, frowning. "If that were the case, why are *you* here?"

"Oh, I thought it was possible Celine mightn't go. She's still carrying the torch for Guy, aren't you, Ceci?"

"I could have sworn you were, too!" Helena looked at her grand-daughter coolly.

"Correct, Gran!" Ashley gave her crack of laughter. "Only this time I have a chance."

"Why don't we go, Ashley?" Celine asked, not wanting to further upset their grandmother's pleasant afternoon. These days Helena wasn't keeping her opinions under lock and key.

"I won't keep her long, Gran," Ashley promised, picking up a swatch of Colefax & Fowler silk taffeta in various colourways and putting it down without comment. "An hour or two. It's Carla Freeman's engagement party tonight. I have to look in. Guy might turn up. Strange you didn't get an invitation, Ceci. Carla used to be very fond of you."

"Maybe you put it about Celine doesn't go where Guy's invited?" Helena said with a crispness that appeared to stagger Ashley.

"*What* did you say, Gran?"

"I happened to run into Carla over a week ago," Celine explained. "She was under that impression."

"We wanted you to know." Helena shook her head severely. "You have a lot of your grandfather in you."

"I take that as a compliment, Gran. I did tell Carla having the two of you together at the same party might upset you. I did it for you, Ceci. I thought you mightn't be able to handle it. Guy *had* to go, of course. He's one of Terry's closest friends."

"In any case it doesn't matter," Celine said smoothly. "I wouldn't miss it for the world."

Once inside Langfield it was hard to tell if Imelda had made an actual improvement. From an overcrowded museum Langfield now looked like an opulent Russian railway station.

"So what do you think?" Ashley asked.

"Splendid! Very...very..." Celine sought but failed to come up with another word. The walls minus the collection seemed to cry out for graffiti.

"Splendid will do. Come up and see my bedroom," Ashley invited. "Suite of rooms, really. I have what was going to be Gran's."

"I expect Grandma thought it was all going to be hers," Celine said, following Ashley up the stairs.

"Anyway it's worked out well. She looks so much better, years younger. I didn't know she had such a sharp tongue."

"Possibly because she had to spend so much time keeping quiet."

"That's never going to happen to me, darling. I hate it the way men try to control you."

Ashley's bedroom was decorated in her own blond and blue colours, with lace bed hangings filtering the morning sunlight. The adjoining room with its leaded-glass windows was used as a luxurious sitting room with a continuation of the blond-and-blue colour scheme.

"Naturally I selected the fabrics," Ashley said casually. "Mamma has been known to go over the top. If I'd left it to her the sitting room would have looked like a compartment on the Orient Express. I'm glad it's finished. I'm looking for new treasures, but nothing could match *this*." She walked to an elegant rosewood desk by the window, picking up a silver gilt-winged female figure that stood near the lamp.

"It's beautiful!" Celine said. And so it was except it had an ambiguous feel to it more erotic than chaste. Perhaps it had something to do with the line of the draperies and the exposed breasts.

"Guy's belated Christmas present to me," Ashley said, her voice pulsing with some secret emotion. "He called it 'Dark Angel'. I suppose it's the way he sees me."

For the first time in her life Celine felt fully prepared to confront her cousin. "Ashley, one day you're going to get hung up on your own lies. Guy didn't give you that. I know that in my bones."

Ashley sighed helplessly. "Ah, Ceci, I was afraid if I told you, you wouldn't believe me. There's part of you that will never accept Guy's no longer yours. Maybe in a weird way he was *never* yours."

"Is this what you got me here for? To show me the statue and tell me Guy gave it to you?"

"No." Ashley smiled at her. "I got you here to talk. We have so much in common."

"But nothing more important than Guy. He *doesn't* love you, Ashley."

"I guess we do have to battle over him." Ashley sat down in an armchair, her ice-blue eyes fixed on Celine's face. "He told me he never stopped thinking about me. What would you call that?"

"Wishful thinking," Celine suggested sharply. "He denies any involvement."

"You mean, you've discussed me?" Ashley's voice crackled with anger. She leaped up from the armchair and went to the window.

"Things have to be settled between us."

"My God!" It came out like a howl. "I've done everything I possibly could to protect you and you betray me?"

"Don't start turning the tables, Ashley," Celine warned. "I know you're very good at it. The betrayal was all on your side."

A long shudder took Ashley's square shoulders. "That's a lie!"

"You love to confuse people," Celine said. "You make up stories. Now that I think about it, you always did."

"How did I ever confuse *you*?" Ashley's ice-blue eyes glittered.

"You deliberately played on all my insecurities to break up my engagement. You wanted me out of the way and you knew that I'd run. You didn't care how much damage you did. Even when you had me safely on the way you tried to destroy my relationship with Grandma.''

"Why would I do an ugly thing like that?" Ashley launched herself away from the window to stand over Celine.

"You've got problems, Ashley. Problems with me."

"With a wimp? Oh, my God, I'm sorry. I didn't mean that. I love you, Ceci. All I've ever done is try and help you."

"You drove me away." Celine said it quietly, simply, a plain statement of fact.

Ashley stood over her, wringing her hands. "Ceci, you were desperate to *get* away. Please take responsibility for your own actions. If I once said you weren't woman enough for Guy I was only articulating your own feelings. Remember when you were little and you lost your voice? I used to say things for you. Remember?"

"I remember our shared history. But somehow, Ashley, you came to resent me. It started *before* Guy, but Guy brought it all to a head. I think you would have tried to take *anyone* I loved off me. It didn't have to be Guy."

"You're talking pure melodrama, Ceci." Ashley brushed a hand across her eyes. "It's indefensible. Everything that's happened to you you did to yourself. You lost Guy because you couldn't match him. You shrunk from it. Now you're trying to take *my* chance from me."

"When you spent so much of your time warning me against him?"

"I knew he'd never make you happy, Ceci. Can't you see that? Guy needs a dynamic kind of woman. A woman who knows her way around the world. You're much too sweet-natured. Admittedly not so vulnerable these days but you don't have my self-assurance. You'd finish up like Gran, living in a man's shadow.''

"Wake up, Ashley. That won't work anymore. For all you've done I still don't want to see you hurt. Guy doesn't love you. He's asked me to marry him.''

For a moment Ashley stood riveted as though trying to grapple with something incomprehensible, then she exploded into sudden rage.

"You're lying!'' she cried, her expression hard and bitter, full of a furious scorn. "Guy's finished with you, hear? Finished. He told me so himself. He could never forgive you for what you did to him.''

"Then it's a measure of his love he still wants me,'' Celine answered, white-faced but resolute.

"This is a trick, Ceci.'' Ashley's blue eyes narrowed to mere slits.

Celine shook her head. "You're the manipulative one, Ashley. You try through your lies to make *your* wishes come true. You lied to me, to Grandma, to Michael, to friends. And for what? Some impossible dream? Guy's a one-woman man and that woman is *me*. Time now to give it all up.''

"And who are you to talk to me?'' Ashley sneered. "You stole everything I ever wanted. I was supposed to feel sorry for you just because your parents had been drowned. So the Titian-haired doll moved into Langfield. With Gramps. He actually preferred you to me. *I* was the first grandchild. The first grand-daughter. But no, you had to have this strange magic about you. Gramps paired you with Guy. It should have been *me*. Guy would have done whatever Gramps wanted. You ruined everything for me. God damn you, Ceci!'' Ashley put her head into her hands and began to sob with a dreadful intensity.

"Ashley, don't!" Celine went to her and grasped her cousin by the arms. "You'll make yourself ill. I'm so very, very sorry about all this. Grandfather had a lot to answer for."

"Let's hope the old devil is burning in hell!" With a movement swift and violent Ashley threw Celine off. She went to the rosewood table, picked up the silver-gilt statue and hurled it with considerable force through the open window.

"Good God, Ashley!" Celine cried in alarm. "Someone could be down there." She made a rush for the window, looking down.

The statue lay almost directly beneath her. It had cleared the line of sasanqua camellias and lay on the thick grass, the tip of one wing buried in the turf, the sun burnishing the silver gilt to a dazzling gold.

Celine groaned aloud with relief. "It's landed on the grass."

"Forget about it," Ashley snapped, going to the dressing table mirror and wiping mascara from beneath one eye.

"It's a mercy no one was around."

"Who would care!" Ashley answered viciously.

"I wouldn't want to be the person to hit your mother on the head."

"I guess the world would roll along without her."

Celine turned back to look at her cousin. "Ashley, don't sound so bitter. You break my heart."

"There you go, so sweet and generous. You make me sick."

At some distance they heard Imelda's voice. Ashley didn't move, as though she had absolutely no intention of opening the door, so Celine crossed the room, admitting an extraordinarily upset-looking Imelda.

"I couldn't believe my eyes!" Imelda looked almost blindly from one to the other. "We were coming up the drive and something came sailing out your window, Ashley. It looked heavy, too."

"It wasn't mine, Mamma." Ashley's answer had the inveterate liar's ring of truth.

"Yours, Celine?" Imelda looked at her niece with confusion. "You really can't do things like that. Somebody could have been hurt."

"It was only fun and games, Mamma."

"It looked totally irresponsible to me." Imelda made a sudden distraught movement, throwing up shaky hands. "That's not what I came to talk to you about. We just heard on the car phone there's been an accident at the Matson site. Someone's been injured or...killed. Pray God it's not the latter. Your father let me off and drove straight back. Are you all right, Celine?" Imelda asked worriedly. "You've gone as white as a sheet."

The room that had tilted, swung back into focus. Celine was experiencing the worst dread she had ever known. No one ever recovered from terrible trauma. The resignation to a crushing fate was always there. "Guy!" she murmured in a near whisper. There was a sensation of bitter cold on her skin.

Something maternal moved Imelda's heart. She went to Celine and put her arm around her. "There was no mention of Guy, dear. Don't let's jump ahead." Still, damp broke out on Imelda's white brow. Almost twenty years but she remembered the dreadful day Guy's father had been killed as though it were yesterday.

"I must go. I must see what's happening." Celine's expression was torn with a terrible anxiety. "Guy's the senior architect. He could be on call."

"I'll drive you," Ashley offered.

How strange her voice sounded!

"I'll come, too," said Imelda. "Better to know than remain here with our worries."

"You won't be needed, Mamma." Ashley turned on her mother almost fiercely.

The distressed Imelda was furiously jolted. "How *dare* you, Ashley?" she thundered. "Sometimes I think I failed badly with you. Don't tell *me* whether I'm needed or not. You forget yourself. Let's go!"

It took them half an hour of speeding to reach the Matson site; an office block high-rise. Celine was too desperately worried to care much about Ashley's driving, but Imelda called out several times a cruising police car would surely pull them over. No one, but no one, was this lucky.

In the event, they were. The city slumbered in the late Saturday afternoon heat.

"Something tells me it's bad trouble!" Ashley muttered. Jaw tight, she ran a red light then turned downtown.

Even three intersections away they could see the flashing lights. Police cars, a fire engine, an ambulance, people standing in little groups in the street. The area had been blocked off. A young policeman held up a warning hand, clearly expecting to be obeyed, but Ashley made her own decision. She swept up to the back bumper of a parked police car and braked just short of hitting it.

"You're a dreadful driver, Ashley," her mother said, breathing fast.

"I got you here, didn't I?"

"You can't stay here, miss!" The policeman walked towards them as though Ashley might start up again at any moment. Even ram the police car.

"Can't I?" Ashley muttered, looking hard and tense.

"Please don't cause trouble, Ashley," Imelda begged. She opened the door of the car and stepped out in her normal regal style.

"Oh, it's *you*, Mrs. Langton," the policeman said in obvious relief. Imelda Langton was almost daily in the papers. He recognised her.

"What is it? What's happening?" Imelda shaded her eyes, looking up.

There was no need to ask. A man stood at the extreme edge of the scaffolding some thirteen floors up. The sway on his body and his dangerous position heralded imminent disaster. Another man had eased out to a few feet away obviously in the hope of talking the man back to safety.

Celine swallowed convulsively. "It's Guy!" She hadn't missed his blue Jaguar parked in the street.

The policeman glanced at her quickly, responding to her agonised tone. "Mr. Harcourt offered to try to talk the man down. He's already broken a mate's nose. He's been threatening to jump for some time. Somehow Mr. Harcourt has managed to keep him there. Family breakup. We're trying to contact the wife, but with no success so far."

"What about a psychiatrist?" Ashley asked harshly.

"One's coming, miss," the policeman said pleasantly, thinking this one was a real charmer. "I don't think he could do a better job than Mr. Harcourt. The fellow knows him well. Worked for Harcourt Langton for years. Yugoslavian, I believe.''

Clive Langton disengaged himself from his group to come back to them. "Bad business," he said, giving Celine the kindest look she had ever received from him. "Poor devil has simply cracked up. We've had a few worries with him but no one wanted to sack him. Guy's managed to get him fairly calm. Or calm compared to what he was."

"He could take Guy with him when he falls," Ashley pointed out harshly.

Clive looked shaken. "It was Guy's decision. God knows I didn't want to put him at risk. We've had our differences, but he's almost *family*." He broke off as the man began to call out in an excited voice.

The small crush of onlookers fell back as though expecting a body to come hurtling at them.

"What's he saying?" Imelda moaned, her face paper white.

"The fool!" Ashley's body shook with violent temper. "If he wants to jump, *let* him!"

"Don't you dare say that!" Clive looked appalled. "He's a good man. He's lost his children and he's been worried sick about them. Where's your heart, Ashley?"

"Don't you *know*?" Ashley was nearly dancing in her rage. "It's up there with Guy."

Anger gave way to pity as Clive realised what his daughter was saying. "I should have stopped this years ago," he said bleakly. "There's no other woman in the world for Guy, but Celine. It's always been Celine, my poor child."

"Quiet. Please be quiet!" Celine implored. She was ready to surrender Guy forever if it would only keep him alive. He was far too close to the edge. Far too close to a dangerously unstable man.

One tragedy too many, Celine thought. This will be one tragedy more than I can possibly bear.

She bowed her head and began to pray. If God failed her...if God failed her...

During the next ten minutes a psychiatrist arrived but decided not to intervene at that point, because Guy Harcourt was doing as good a job as anyone could hope for. The distraught man had quietened. He had even waved to the crowd in the street and amazingly they had all waved back. Except Celine, who was shaking with nerves.

The policeman suddenly exclaimed. "He's got him. Bewdy! He's actually got him."

Clive Langton grunted his intense relief. "Looks like it. This isn't my idea of a peaceful Saturday afternoon, being half frightened to death. We'll have to help this poor fella!"

The man came quietly, apparently drained of all resolve. As he was led out onto the street by the police, a patrol car pulled up, discharging the estranged wife. She jumped out, then suddenly hurled herself at her husband whether in anger or relief Celine couldn't say.

She only had eyes for Guy. The police chief was thumping him on the back, probably commending him for his courage. Guy lifted a hand, then walked on, fending off questions from the press.

"We might as well go home now, Ashley," Imelda said quietly to her daughter.

Ashley's lips twisted into a bruised smile. "I suppose even I have to accept the inevitable."

"Yes, darling." Imelda nodded soberly.

Celine kept on walking until she was locked in Guy's waiting arms. It was a marvellous, intimate moment that said very clearly what was in their hearts.

"If I *lost* you," Celine murmured, her face buried against his chest.

"Not even death could separate us," he said. "I love you, Celine. I love you with all my heart."

"Let's go home," she said, lifting her face and staring into his eyes.

"Home?" He smiled a little quizzically.

"To *your* place," she said. "Your little penthouse in the sky."

"You know the first thing I'm going to do to you, don't you?" His beautiful dark eyes fairly blazed, revealing the depth of his exultation.

"I'll settle for making love all night!" Celine's pale cheeks were flushed to sudden radiance.

"It's a deal!"

It wasn't said flippantly, but with an intensity to take her breath away.

A photograph appeared in the following morning's paper. It was brilliant, touching. It caused much comment. The camera had caught lovingly two young people utterly focused on each other. The caption read,

A Harcourt Langton Merger?

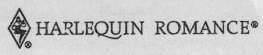

HARLEQUIN ROMANCE®

brings you

Romances that take the family to heart!

Coming next month from Jessica Steele is
THE SISTER SECRET (#3385), our Family Ties book
for November. The "tie" here is rather special—Belvia
and Josy are twin sisters!

But though they look alike, they're chalk and cheese when
it comes to their characters. Josy has always been painfully
shy, while Belvia...well, she isn't afraid of speaking her
mind.

When sisters are in a tight spot they stick together. Josy
has a secret that Belvia is determined to keep. And that
means keeping Josy away from Latham Tavenner.
Unfortunately, the family firm needs Latham's help. Belvia
has no alternative than to attract Latham's attention.
Latham knows exactly which sister he wants. But he's not
about to let Belvia know that!

Look out for Josy's story in A WIFE IN WAITING,
coming soon from Harlequin Romance.

OFFICIAL RULES

PRIZE SURPRISE SWEEPSTAKES 3448

NO PURCHASE OR OBLIGATION NECESSARY

Three Harlequin Reader Service 1995 shipments will contain respectively, coupons for entry into three different prize drawings, one for a Panasonic 31" wide-screen TV, another for a 5-piece Wedgwood china service for eight and the third for a Sharp ViewCam camcorder. To enter any drawing using an Entry Coupon, simply complete and mail according to directions.

There is no obligation to continue using the Reader Service to enter and be eligible for any prize drawing. You may also enter any drawing by hand printing the words "Prize Surprise," your name and address on a 3"x5" card and the name of the prize you wish that entry to be considered for (i.e., Panasonic wide-screen TV, Wedgwood china or Sharp ViewCam). Send your 3"x5" entries via first-class mail (limit: one per envelope) to: Prize Surprise Sweepstakes 3448, c/o the prize you wish that entry to be considered for, P.O. Box 1315, Buffalo, NY 14269-1315, USA or P.O. Box 610, Fort Erie, Ontario L2A 5X3, Canada.

To be eligible for the Panasonic wide-screen TV, entries must be received by 6/30/95; for the Wedgwood china, 8/30/95; and for the Sharp ViewCam, 10/30/95.

Winners will be determined in random drawings conducted under the supervision of D.L. Blair, Inc., an independent judging organization whose decisions are final, from among all eligible entries received for that drawing. Approximate prize values are as follows: Panasonic wide-screen TV ($1,800); Wedgwood china ($840) and Sharp ViewCam ($2,000). Sweepstakes open to residents of the U.S. (except Puerto Rico) and Canada, 18 years of age or older. Employees and immediate family members of Harlequin Enterprises, Ltd., D.L. Blair, Inc., their affiliates, subsidiaries and all other agencies, entities and persons connected with the use, marketing or conduct of this sweepstakes are not eligible. Odds of winning a prize are dependent upon the number of eligible entries received for that drawing. Prize drawing and winner notification for each drawing will occur no later than 15 days after deadline for entry eligibility for that drawing. Limit: one prize to an individual, family or organization. All applicable laws and regulations apply. Sweepstakes offer void wherever prohibited by law. Any litigation within the province of Quebec respecting the conduct and awarding of the prizes in this sweepstakes must be submitted to the Regies des loteries et Courses du Quebec. In order to win a prize, residents of Canada will be required to correctly answer a time-limited arithmetical skill-testing question. Value of prizes are in U.S. currency.

Winners will be obligated to sign and return an Affidavit of Eligibility within 30 days of notification. In the event of noncompliance within this time period, prize may not be awarded. If any prize or prize notification is returned as undeliverable, that prize will not be awarded. By acceptance of a prize, winner consents to use of his/her name, photograph or other likeness for purposes of advertising, trade and promotion on behalf of Harlequin Enterprises, Ltd., without further compensation, unless prohibited by law.

For the names of prizewinners (available after 12/31/95), send a self-addressed, stamped envelope to: Prize Surprise Sweepstakes 3448 Winners, P.O. Box 4200, Blair, NE 68009.

RPZ KAL